"Penny for them," a voice said

Camilla was startled. She looked up, parrying the cool inquiry of Quinn's glance with a protective gleam of irony.

"I was wishing that I was small and pretty and outgoing," she said.

His brows lifted in somewhat mocking surprise as he surveyed every inch of her length at leisure and with narrowed gaze. When he had finished she was pink-cheeked and her eyes were glittering like affronted jewels.

"Why?" His tone was sardonic. "I prefer subtlety. You are just the right height for ... conversation."

He smiled teasingly as the color glowed through her skin. He had been going to say, "for kissing"—she just knew it!

ROBYN DONALD lives in northern New Zealand with her husband and children. They love the outdoors and particularly enjoy sailing and stargazing on warm nights. Robyn doesn't remember being taught to read, but rates reading as one of her greatest pleasures, if not a vice. She finds writing intensely rewarding and is continually surprised by the way her characters develop independent lives of their own.

Books by Robyn Donald

ROBYN DONALD

no guarantees

Harlequin Books

TORONTO • NEW YORK • LONDON
AMSTERDAM • PARIS • SYDNEY • HAMBURG
STOCKHOLM • ATHENS • TOKYO • MILAN

Harlequin Presents first edition October 1990
ISBN 0-373-11303-X

Original hardcover edition published in 1990
by Mills & Boon Limited

CHAPTER ONE

CAMILLA heard the telephone just as she turned the tap on over the tub in the wash-house. For a moment she hesitated; one call sign sounded much like another on the antiquated party-line system which the district of Bowden was almost the last in New Zealand to suffer, and the two long rings signifying her number were easily confused with the one short and two longs that denoted Falls homestead.

Still, she was expecting a call, so she wrenched the tap closed and flew inside, grabbing the receiver with cold, wet hands.

'189M,' she said breathlessly.

'Wrong number, Mrs Evans.'

The voice was deep, sharpened by a hint of sarcasm that made Camilla flush as she jerked out a flustered apology before slamming the receiver down. It would have to be Quinn Fraser who was on the other end. Just as it had been Quinn who was the first along the road when the bull had got out and held up the school bus. And Quinn who had arrived first on the scene when Dave had rolled the tractor and died beneath it.

The doctor had told her that although she would always feel grief the worst would be over after a year. And yesterday was the first anniversary of Dave's death.

It seemed like a lifetime, but the doctor had been right. However, he probably would have been as shocked as Camilla to realise that, although she had grieved long and deeply over Dave's death, her grief had been more for his loss, the abrupt severance of his life before he'd had a chance to accomplish all that he was capable of, than for her own sake.

Guiltily she pushed the thought away. Whatever Dave and she had shared might not have been the love of the century, but it had been satisfying in its way. They had both had a commitment to the farm that should have been enough for her, and certainly Dave had never queried her love for him.

Slowly she went back into the wash-house and turned on the taps again. She had been appalled when first she had seen this room, with its unpainted walls and the detritus of years in various corners. In spite of Dave's objections she had bought paint out of the housekeeping money and stolen the time to repaint. It still showed its age, but the pretty, cheerful colour lifted her spirits every time she went into it.

Breakfast was a grapefruit from the huge old tree out in the yard, followed by toast and a cup of tea while she read the headlines in yesterday's newspaper. Once she caught herself yawning, and looked up guiltily before she could stop herself, because Dave used to get angry if she appeared at all tired. He had hated it when their shaky finances had meant that she had to work part time for the market gardener down the road. In spite of the fact that he also was forced to work for a contractor, digging drains and spraying, it had hurt his prickly male pride, making him unreasonable and over-protective, so she had got into the habit of hiding any signs of exhaustion.

She had just finished her cup of tea when the telephone went again, definitely her number this time.

'Camilla?'

'Yes, Guy?' Her smile showed in her voice.

'I've been trying to get you, but the line's been busy. Do you still want to go to this sale?'

'I do,' she said fervently. An electrical fence unit had been advertised and she badly needed one. As there was no way she could afford a new unit, she had pinned her hopes on this opportunity. However, a note in his pleasant voice warned her of a hitch. She braced herself.

Sure enough, he said, 'I'm sorry, but I can't go. I've just had a ring from the lawyer and I'll have to see him this morning. I can't get out of it, I'm afraid.'

'It's all right, don't worry, don't give it another thought. Of course you must go. My car——'

'You will not go out to Tangaroa in that delapidated thing,' he interrupted. 'It sounds like a chainsaw. The road is too rough for you to even think of taking it. I've organised another ride for you.'

Cautiously, because she hated to be beholden to anyone, she said, 'That's very kind of you.'

He chuckled. 'You won't think so when you hear that it's Quinn Fraser.'

After a silent, horrified second, Camilla responded stiffly, 'I'd rather not——'

'Listen, just because Dave found it necessary to carry on that stupid feud of your uncle's, there's no need for you to do it too. I don't know how your uncle got offside with Quinn, but although I had a lot of time for Dave I thought he was being ridiculous to refuse to have anything to do with the biggest landowner in the district! Loyalty to the memory of the dead is one thing, wilfully cutting off your nose to spite your face is another. Quinn wasn't even at the homestead for most of your marriage! He spent a year overseas with that government trade mission! This is New Zealand, not some barbaric place rampant with vendettas, and Quinn's an honest man.'

'Quinn Fraser,' Camilla said deliberately, 'is an arrogant, superior, nasty-tongued autocrat with a per-

verted sense of humour. I don't know why Uncle Philip
fell out with him, but it was enough to——' She bit back
the precipitate words. Horrified by the anger that had
made her lose control, she finished swiftly, 'I'm sorry,
Guy. I've had a bad night, I'm afraid.'

His voice softened. 'Yes, I know. It's a sad anniversary for you, poor old thing. Don't worry, I won't
tell our local magnate your opinion of him. But you will
accept a lift from him, won't you? I really don't like to
think of you out on the road in that rattletrap of yours.'

Until the cheque from the Dairy Company was paid
into her bank account she wouldn't have enough money
to fill the tank with petrol. If she wanted to get to that
sale it would have to be with Quinn Fraser. In a tone
she hoped didn't sound as falsely cheerful as it was, she
said, 'Yes, I'll go with him. Thank you for arranging
it.'

'Good. He'll pick you up at nine-thirty. And try to
remember, Camilla, that he's only a man. He may look
like a Greek god and behave like one, too, all concentrated masculinity and the kind of arrogance that's so
inborn that it isn't really arrogance, but if you cut him
he bleeds, just like the rest of us.'

Which might well be true, but Guy was so kind that
he would never be able to understand a man like Quinn.

And what makes you think you do? she jeered silently.
After all, everyone who knows him thinks he's absolutely wonderful. Why should you be so convinced that
beneath that sophisticated exterior there's a barbarian?
You don't even know the man very well!

She had to sink her pride and go to the sale with a
man whom her husband had hated because otherwise
she could not afford an electric fence. And if she didn't
get a new one, the land that her husband had loved more
than anything else—apart from her—would suffer.

A glance at the cheap boy's watch on her thin wrist made her whistle soundlessly between her teeth and fly into action. There was just time for a quick shower in the tiny, old-fashioned bathroom before changing into something a little more suitable for the exalted company she was about to keep.

Not that she had much to choose from. There had been no spare money for clothes since her marriage. But she didn't need a large selection of clothes—Bowden was a farming district, and, apart from the rarefied regions that Quinn Fraser occupied, the social life was informal. With a wry twist of her generous mouth, she finally donned trousers of a sensible lovat green, lightened by a pale gold shirt and a deeper green jacket of suede, all relics from the days when she had earned a reasonable wage as a legal secretary in Auckland.

Gazing disparagingly at her reflection, she sighed. Oh, the jacket and trousers suited her long legs and wide shoulders, but they were hardly glamorous. After a moment's frowning survey, she fossicked about in her drawer until she found a small, well-used pot of blusher. It would at least give her face some colour. Not that it mattered; no one would be looking very hard at her.

Dispassionately she itemised her looks: palest grey eyes set slantwise in thick, straight black lashes; a cap of straight black hair, glossy as a pool beneath a moonlit sky; a wide, firm mouth, very red; high, stark cheekbones; milk-white skin that never tanned, with seven gold freckles across her straight nose. The rest was average: a reasonable figure, too slim but surprisingly strong, and long, slender bones. She didn't see the erect, graceful carriage, or that there was a wealth of obstinacy in her square chin, at that moment defiantly lifted.

'You are just staring at yourself because Quinn is always seen with lusciously beautiful creatures and you haven't a single voluptuous curve,' she said scornfully, turning away as though the sight hurt her.

The rattle of a car crossing the cattle-grid banished her reverie, bringing an unaccustomed heat burning across her cheeks. Muttering beneath her breath about stupid women, she grabbed a scarf, a pair of sun-glasses and her bag, and fled.

By the time the car came to a stop outside the gate she was half-way down the narrow path that bisected the small front lawn, but even so Quinn had the gate open before she got there, muscles flexing beneath the material of his shirt as he wrenched the reluctant thing wide and thrust it back again when she had gone through.

Guy had compared him to a Greek god, but Camilla didn't think there was much resemblance. Those creatures had always struck her as being rather mindless slaves to their senses, and the first thing she had noticed about Quinn Fraser was the cool, alert intelligence that overshadowed his stunning masculinity. And the powerful sense of purpose, as though there was nothing he couldn't do because he was completely in control of his mind and his emotions and his will.

Was he handsome? It didn't matter. He was all man, made infinitely dangerous by an air of elegant arrogance and total mastery of himself and anything else that came his way. Hair the colour of wet chestnuts gleamed in the autumn sun; his eyes were green and opaque as they surveyed her with a bland, thoroughly infuriating assessment.

Virile as ever, she thought savagely, giving him a constricted smile.

'Good morning, Camilla.' His voice was a nice blend of calculated irony and amusement. As he opened the car door for her, he said, 'I'll send someone over to fix the hinges of that gate.'

She said calmly, 'No, thank you. It's very rarely used. Most people know to come to the back door.'

He lifted a finely etched brow at her, but said nothing as he shut the door with a gentle thunk. His car even sounded rich, she thought morosely, as she surveyed the gleaming leather and wood interior of the Jaguar. Didn't he know there was a recession on, and the pastoral sector was harder hit than most? Her capable fingers seemed to have lost their deftness as she fumbled with the seat-belt. No, local gossip insisted that he had irons in an assortment of fires both here and overseas; 'recession' was probably only a word to him.

Whereas for her—but she would not think of the rapidly climbing interest rates on the mortgage repayments.

Her skin prickled as he slid in beside her. For all his size, which was considerable, he moved with the purposeful litheness of a great beast of prey. Grimly she concentrated on her recalcitrant seat-belt. However, it remained uncooperative; after fiddling with it for some moments she was finally forced to ask in a polite but goaded voice. 'How does this work?'

'Like this.' He pulled his across his chest and clipped it into the slot.

Camilla tried to copy, but hers balked again.

'Let me.' He did not touch her as he guided it into place and pushed it home, but she was all too conscious of his hands, which were lean and well-shaped and far too close to her shrinking torso.

How ridiculous to be put at any sort of disadvantage by this man just because he looked like the hero of every fevered romance she had read during her adolescence! Or was it that effortless air of authority, that cool, unshakeable confidence that had so infuriated and antagonised Dave?

'Are you comfortable?' he asked with smooth politeness as the car pulled out on to the road.

'Very, thank you.'

And that was all that was said until he had negotiated the five miles of gravel road that lay between them and the sealed highway.

Then, after efficiently passing one of the enormous trucks that collected whole milk from dairy farms like Camilla's all over the country, he observed with an undertone of taunting humour, 'We still have thirty miles to go, Camilla. If you prefer it I'll remain silent all the way, but I can see no reason why we shouldn't talk. On uncontroversial subjects, of course,' he finished affably.

Irritated embarrassment prickled between her shoulders, but she managed to reply in tones as level as his, 'I haven't taken a vow of silence. I thought perhaps you needed to concentrate on your driving.'

To her surprise, he chuckled, slanting her a genuinely amused smile. 'You don't miss an opportunity, do you?'

Which took the wind out of her sails completely. He took his charm so completely for granted that it didn't grate, although it was unfair that one man should have so much. It must make life so much easier for him.

Usually her defences were sound. Today, that lurking smile won an answering one from her. 'I'm sorry,' she said, astounded at herself. 'That was rude and quite untrue. I know you're a good driver.'

Silence was suddenly a barrier between them. In both their minds was the memory of that nightmare trip to the hospital behind the ambulance, a drive that had ended in Dave's death.

After a moment he said, 'Exactly a year ago, wasn't it?'

'Yesterday.' Unconsciously her chin lifted as she stared ahead through the windscreen at the crisp autumn day.

'My mother sends her regards. You knew she was back?'

'Yes.' Mrs Fraser had spent much of the previous year in Hawaii nursing her mother. Quinn had been there for a lot of the time, too. Diffidently she went on, 'I was sorry to hear of your grandmother's death.'

He said without expression, 'She was old and tired, more than ready to go.' And without waiting for a comment he went on, 'My mother would like to call in and see you one day. I hope you won't allow the disagreements we've had to colour your welcome of her.'

She bit her lip. He was referring to Dave, who had resented Mrs Fraser's kind attempts to introduce them to the district social life. Stiffly, because it seemed like disloyalty, she responded, 'Of course I won't. I'll be very happy to see her again.'

'I'm glad.' For once his words were without the mockery that almost always underlaid his beautiful voice.

Camilla looked away. Too susceptible to that rare sincerity, she concentrated on the scenery, surprised by the effort it took. The road began to wind up the side of one of the ancient volcanoes that dotted the landscape. Above, great crags of solidified lava towered grey and purple, bare against the mellow autumn sky, but below them were vivid green paddocks polka-dotted with sheep. On the eastern horizon glimmered the sea, a shining silver plate curving at the edges. Farmhouses nestled among trees and gardens still gay with chrysanthemums and dahlias and the subtle pink and rose of early sasanqua camellias.

'The country looks good,' Camilla said impulsively, her spirits rising. She had forgotten how pleasant it was to get away from the ever-present worries of the farm.

'Yes. This has been the best autumn for growth in twenty years,' he observed, adding, 'We could be in for a bout of facial eczema. Have you had any signs of it? It's still warm enough for the fungus to grow.'

'Not a sign so far.'

'Taken any precautions?'

Precautions cost money. 'I'm not entirely stupid,' she said, all the more indignant because she was lying by implication and she was normally a truthful person. But she was watching the cows with an eagle eye for symptoms.

His wide shoulders lifted in the slightest of shrugs. 'Why do you take umbrage so quickly? I know you're almost completely new to dairying, but surely the three years you've spent farming have shown you that people in the country are interdependent, that we help each other? Farmers who have lived on the land all their lives accept advice.'

'I don't need help. I'm managing.'

'It's only my help that you don't want. Independence is an admirable trait, but letting your dislike override your common sense is stupidity, and there's nothing admirable about that.' His voice was hard and level and slightly scornful. 'If Guy Sorrell hadn't jacked up this ride you'd have stayed at home rather than ask me, wouldn't you?'

She said quietly, 'I didn't know you were going.'

A glance like a rapier slid over her face. After a moment he said, 'At least give me credit for some neighbourly feelings. I admire your determination, the way you've kept things going. If you need help, will you come to me?'

Camilla dithered. Oh, he knew how to persuade; in the deep voice there was only concern, but Uncle Philip had mistrusted Quinn so much that he had only left her the farm on condition that she never sell it to him. And

Dave had resented and disliked him. To accept his help seemed like the greatest disloyalty to both of them.

She said in a muted voice, 'I honestly don't see that you can do much for me. I—thank you for offering. It's very kind of you.'

He gave a short, unamused laugh. 'I can be kind. Useful, too, on occasions of life and death.'

Her skin paled, but she said nothing. When she had heard Dave scream as the tractor went over she had rung the Fraser homestead even before she had raced along to the hillside where her husband had lain beneath the piece of machinery. And Quinn had been there almost immediately with his men, organising them to lift the tractor from Dave's poor broken body, working like a madman himself, all feuds and animosities obliterated in the effort to save a life. He had been so kind, driving her to the hospital behind the wailing ambulance, and afterwards, when it was all over, comforting her as well as he could before bringing her back to his mother.

But then, everyone had been wonderful. It was all the more astonishing because Dave's difficult temperament had antagonised many of them. The neighbouring farmers had organised a roster to milk the cows and do the chores around the farm. When she had refused to sell to Quinn, most of them had thought she was crazy, but they had gone on helping until she was able to take over herself.

The Frasers had been incredibly good to her, too, in those first terrifying weeks. Which made her wonder, for about the thousandth fruitless time, just why her uncle had made that condition in his will. What had Quinn done to Philip Harmsworth to extend his hatred beyond the grave?

Quinn was universally admired and respected, and not, she had to admit, because he was by far the biggest landowner for miles around. It was his character that won esteem from his extremely independent peers, the farmers of the district.

'That,' he said, 'was uncalled for. I'm sorry.'

Bewildered, she stared up at him, some detached part of her brain noting the strikingly aristocratic slash of his profile, almost fiercely chiselled from bone and muscle. 'I—oh!' He was referring to the last time she had called on his help, literally a matter of life and death. 'It's all right,' she said in a stifled voice.

Unexpectedly his hand dropped over her tense ones, closed on them for a moment, then was replaced on the wheel. 'Do you still grieve for him?' She flinched and he said instantly, 'I'm sorry, Camilla. I didn't mean to probe.'

His touch had thrown her completely off balance. The words came without volition. 'I miss him still.'

Her husband's death had shocked and saddened her, but long before Dave had been killed she had accepted that her romantic dreams of a lifelong passion, two people who were all in all to each other, had been just that—dreams. She had married for all the wrong reasons, and because she couldn't bear to hurt him she had packed those dreams away and settled for what she had.

Dave had not been easy to live with, but he had been a good man and Camilla had been brought up to believe that promises were to be kept. She had hoped that children would help, their shared interest in the land—and it would have been enough, she told herself fiercely.

'Poor Camilla. You've had a lot of grief in your twenty-two years, haven't you? I believe both your parents are dead.' There was an unusual note in the deep voice, not exactly sympathy, more—anger?

'Yes.' Her jaw tightened as she turned her head to stare sightlessly out of the side window. Perhaps loneliness was another of the reasons she had clung to the marriage. That, and the knowledge that if she left Dave she would be shutting him out from his only chance to fulfil his one ambition, work his own farm.

Coming from a poor family, one of many children, he had left school at the earliest possible date and worked at a reasonably well-paid job with no future, a job he had hated. He had no chance of acquiring either the capital to buy or the skills to work on the land until Philip Harmsworth had died and left Camilla the farm. Grief-stricken by the death of her mother, at first she had wanted to sell it, but Dave, who had been slowly turning from the boy next door to the man in her life, had persuaded her that they could make a go of it.

Aloud she said, 'My shoulders are pretty wide. I can take it.'

Anger was replaced by the much more familiar mockery. 'You don't allow anyone to feel sorry for you, do you?'

'It weakens me.' Now, why on earth had she said that?

'And you can't have that. You have to prove that you're as tough as the next man.' He slanted her another look, green and glittering. 'Unfortunately, in spite of those broad shoulders, the rest of your feminine attributes do not bring to mind any sort of tough farmer. My mother says you're the only person she knows who makes jeans and gumboots and a bush shirt look feminine.'

The compliment brought a runaway colour to her cheeks. Still staring through the window, she said stiffly, 'That's very kind of her. Your mother is a darling.'

'It runs in the family,' he said teasingly.

Camilla's smile was strained. Quinn was very much a man; he made any woman instantly aware of her 'feminine attributes', and Camilla was no exception. Most emphatically she did not want the conversation to drift around to personalities. She had already revealed more than she should to him.

Fortunately their turning came up almost immediately. Theirs was not the only vehicle on the road, and to Camilla's relief he had to concentrate on guiding them through a thick cloud of dust. Once a car overtook them, cutting back in too sharply. Quinn said nothing, although the classically moulded line of his mouth compressed as he had to brake. He dropped back to leave a safe distance between them and the car in front.

Camilla couldn't help comparing this reaction to Dave's in similar situations. Cursed with a quick fuse, he used to stamp viciously on the brakes, jerking the vehicle about the road and driving far too close behind to signify his displeasure, muttering profanities under his breath.

After several miles of slow progress they turned into a paddock beside an enormous modern house overlooking a lagoon at the mouth of a small river. The wind nipped in from the south, ruffling massive puriri trees that crouched in the grass. When she got out, Camilla shivered, and Quinn instantly leaned into the car and picked up her suede jacket, holding it for her to shrug into. His hands rested a moment on her shoulders. A tingle, like a charge of electricity, sizzled through her. Swiftly she moved away.

He didn't seem to notice the rebuff. As they set off towards the area where the sale was to be held he took her arm. It meant nothing; she had seen him do it before with the same automatic courtesy, but her body's swift, dazzled reaction frightened her.

It was this fear that enabled her to say calmly, 'You don't have to stay with me, Quinn. There must be people you want to talk to.'

His fingers tightened fractionally as he replied with cool deliberation, 'There are, but I can see no reason for you to skulk around by yourself like an uninvited guest.'

She could, of course, tell him that she preferred to be alone. It was the truth. It would also be extremely rude. 'Oh, I—no.'

If he noticed her momentary hesitation he didn't remark on it. 'Right. Now, do you want to have a look at this fence unit? It will be over here in the shed.'

Her reaction to his powerful personality had totally swamped her reason for being there. It was an ominous realisation. Very stiffly she said, 'Yes, of course.'

On the way they were handed catalogues by a thin young man whose swift, shrewd perusal of her face and figure brought a fugitive sparkle to Camilla's pale eyes. Without much difficulty she subdued her temper. It didn't matter what anyone thought about her presence on Quinn Fraser's arm. His usual women were far too sophisticated and elegant for her to be mistaken for one.

But when it became clear that half of Bowden, complete with spouse, was there, startled and interested in the fact that he was escorting her, Camilla began to think that she should have insisted on making her way independently. As in all small country districts, gossip ranged wide and enthusiastically. She hated the thought of being coupled with him in any way.

In the past few months there had been several uncomfortable incidents that had warned her of some men's assumptions about widows—mainly the limitless lust that was attributed to them. Those memories still made her blood boil, and the last thing she wanted to do was give anyone the idea that she was in the market for an affair.

Comforting herself with the fact that one day in Quinn's company could hardly ruin her reputation, she was still acutely conscious of the ripples of conjecture that followed them into the shed.

The fence was a good one, almost new. To her surprise Quinn checked it carefully, his expression absorbed as he bent over it. He obviously knew what he was doing, but then, she thought waspishly, he would. He had that air of competence. There was a mechanic on the station whose job was to look after all the machinery there, but she was prepared to believe that Quinn would be just as efficient and knowledgeable as his employee.

She recalled ruefully some of the struggles she had had with machinery on the farm. If she ever had a daughter, she would make sure she could find her way around a toolkit.

'It's in good condition,' he told her, interrupting her thoughts. He smiled at her startled face and named a price, saying, 'I wouldn't go above that for it, myself.'

It was more than she had expected to spend, but with a little belt-tightening here and there she would be able to manage it. And it would save her enough to make the day off work a worthwhile investment.

Unconsciously she sighed, her eyes darkening. Money! If only the farm were twenty acres bigger. If only Dave hadn't borrowed from the bank to put in a new herringbone milking shed when they had first come. If only the interest rates hadn't sky-rocketed. If only...

Sometimes Camilla felt that she had never had a moment free from worries about money. In the two years that she had spent working before she had married, her wages had had to stretch to cover the costs of an invalid mother. But at least the decisions had been hers. Her mother had encouraged her to buy clothes chosen because they looked good on her, not for their utility and wearing qualities. She had managed to save for books, and records...

From above Quinn said, in a casual voice at variance with the piercing green glance that met her shadowed eyes, 'Too much?'

'No,' she said, and more sturdily, 'No, that's about what I expected to pay. What are you planning to buy?'

'Some yearling beasts. Come and have a look at them.'

Gladly, she went with him, pleased to have something else to occupy her mind. As the cattle stamped and bawled and shifted around in the crowded pens, they rolled wary, suspicious eyes. Although not yet fully grown, they would be expensive. Wistfully she wondered what it would be like to have enough money to afford to buy a pen of the beasts.

'Camilla?' When she looked blankly into his face he smiled gently and ran a long, tanned forefinger down between her brows. 'That's an exceptionally ferocious frown.'

Those eyes saw too much. Taking a breath that had to fight its way past an obstruction in her throat, she improvised hastily as she stepped away. 'I was just thinking that one of those would fill my deep-freeze rather nicely. If it were empty,' she added positively and barely truthfully, 'which it is not.'

He lifted a dark eyebrow—whether at her words or the pointed way she moved away from his touch, she didn't know—and said without expression, 'They're about to start.'

Had she been with Guy, Camilla would have enjoyed herself immensely. As it was, by a considerable exertion of will she managed to relax enough to take pleasure in the silver and blue day, the crisp, autumnal scents borne by the cool wind, the high-pitched, monotonous and incredibly fast delivery of the auctioneer, his henchmen shouting as they took bids from around the crowd. The sun shone down, mitigating the breeze, and below them the river sparkled on its way to the wider glitter of the sea. An upwelling of delight lifted her mood, and when Quinn smiled at her she smiled back, her expression open and guileless.

Something darkened the hard opacity of his eyes; his mouth pulled in and a small muscle flicked beside the strong line of his jaw. Camilla's breath stopped in her throat, but his voice was completely impersonal as he said, 'Your lot's coming next. Do you want me to bid for you?'

'No, thank you.' She managed to grin. 'I've never bid at an auction, and I'm rather looking forward to it. Stop me if I get carried away and go on past my limit.'

He laughed down at her, the magnetism very blatant. 'I think you're altogether too level-headed to succumb to that particular fever. However, if I see any sign of madness, I'll clap my hand over your mouth.'

Her glance fell to his hands. Lean-fingered, tanned, they were more than capable of physically silencing her. She had a momentary vision of them, dark and strong against the transparent pallor of her skin, and swallowed, appalled at the flicker of forbidden excitement it aroused in her.

Avoiding his eyes, she turned away and said tonelessly, 'Yes, you do that.'

But when the fence unit came up only two other people bid for it, and they dropped out quite quickly, so that the auctioneer pointed to her and said, 'Sold to Mrs Evans.'

Elated, because she hadn't had to go to her limit, she beamed up at Quinn. 'When can I pick it up?'

'Do you want it straight away?'

The distant tone put a complete damper on her pleasure. Her eyes widened, then slid past his face to fix on a point just beyond his shoulder. Matching her tone to his, she replied, 'As soon as possible.'

'Pay one of the attendants. I'll put it in the car.'

'But what about your beasts?'

'They don't come up until after lunch.'

When they came back to the ring it was to find the auction temporarily disbanded for the greater attractions of food. Camilla was looking about for the lunch tent when a man hailed Quinn. It was the owner of the property, a middle-aged man with a thatch of reddish hair and a cultured voice. He insisted they go up to the house for lunch—'just sandwiches, as Nadine's away'— and was sweetly gallant to Camilla, of whom he had clearly heard.

Already made sensitive by the none too subtle interest their arrival together had caused, she braced herself for more, but he was a sophisticated man, and gave no indication of anything more than a slightly old-fashioned courtesy.

Nevertheless, she was pleased to leave the rarefied company of the rich gentleman farmer, where Quinn was so clearly at home, and go back to the sale.

He bought his beasts, and, after organising their carriage back to Falls, decided that it was time to go. It was a quiet trip back; they spoke little, and that was mostly comments on the sale. When they passed the wide gates that led into Falls she stared up the drive, which was shadowed by an avenue of huge silky oaks. She had been up there only once. Shortly after their marriage, Mrs Fraser had invited them to dinner. It had been a tense occasion, marred by Dave's taciturnity. He'd refused to allow her to return the invitation.

'But why?' she had asked, unsurprised, but determined to discover the reason.

'Because I don't like being patronised, and I'm damned sure your uncle wouldn't have liked to see us sitting up there with damned Fraser behaving like the lord of the manor.'

There had been a note of insecurity in his voice that had silenced her. So she had acceded, and, after a couple of invitations had been refused, Mrs Fraser didn't ask any more.

'Asleep?'

She started at the soft question. 'No. Thinking.'

'Were you expecting a visitor?'

'No.' She stared at him, then dragged her eyes away to look across to her house. 'Why?'

'The taxi has just passed us, and as yours is the only house past the homestead I conclude that he's dropped someone off there. Someone who came on the two-thirty bus from Auckland.'

Camilla said, 'No. I haven't invited anyone...'

Her voice trailed away, because even from this distance she could see someone sitting on the front steps.

Ben's deep barking filled the air with frenzied clamour as the sound of the car engine died. Camilla leapt out, shouting at him to be quiet as she hauled the gate open and ran towards the woman who sat so demurely waiting for her. Red-brown hair styled in the latest geometric cut, an exquisitely made-up face framing sherry-brown eyes...

'Hello, Karen,' Camilla managed, pleasure warming her voice. 'How lovely to see you!'

CHAPTER TWO

GRACEFULLY the older woman climbed to her feet, her eyes fixed on Quinn as he came up the path after Camilla. 'Hi, Cam. Sorry to arrive out of the blue like this.'

Turning, Camilla caught a glimpse of amused interest in the handsome face behind her, and hastily made the introductions. 'This is Quinn Fraser, my neighbour. Quinn, this is my cousin, Karen Parker.'

'How do you do?' The words were impersonal, but he smiled down into Karen's lovely face with unfeigned pleasure.

And she was in no hurry to remove her hand from his grip. 'Hello,' she said demurely.

A strange pang tore through Camilla. On the pretence of silencing the dog, she turned away, calling, 'Quiet, Ben. OK, that's enough!' and stood watching for a wretched few moments until he subsided. Then, pushing back the soft black tendrils of hair that had suddenly settled hot and heavy on her scalp, she banished an ache of foreboding and turned back.

A splendid couple, she thought with an attempt at irony. They looked as if they belonged to the same world—Quinn tall and dark with the long bones and autocratic features of his Celtic ancestors, Karen not even coming up to his shoulder, a dainty, cream-skinned creature with those incredible golden eyes and a mouth passionate with promise. Superbly dressed in a classical twin-set and a fine tweed skirt of pale pink, she breathed sophistication.

Beside her, Camilla felt clumsy and badly dressed. 'Come in, I'll make a pot of tea,' she said crisply.

'I'll wait until I get home, thank you.' Quinn was pleasant, but definite. 'Where shall I put this unit?'

'In the shed.' Too late, she remembered the paucity of equipment and fertiliser there and amended hastily, 'No, don't. I'll take it down when I do the milking.'

'It won't take me a minute——'

'Thanks very much, but leave it here, will you?' She knew that her voice was too sharp, but if he took offence it was just tough luck. She wanted him gone, and quickly.

Showing no anger or annoyance, he removed the unit from the boot of the car and strode with it up the path to set it on the narrow step.

Ashamed, Camilla said gruffly, 'Thank you very much for the lift.'

Mockery gleamed green beneath his lashes. 'My pleasure,' he said smoothly before turning to Karen. 'Enjoy your holiday in Bowden, Karen. I hope we see more of you before you go.'

'I'd like that,' Karen said, with just the right shades of meaning in her tone.

As soon as the car engine started she asked in a vastly different tone, 'Is this the next-door neighbour you've been so reticent about? From the little you wrote I gathered he had horns and cloven hooves—at the very least!' She watched as the big car turned into the driveway to Falls. A low whistle made Camilla look up. 'So that's where he lives. You can't see much of it from the road, but it looks huge.'

'Yes, that's Falls homestead. And it is huge.' To forestall any further comment, Camilla picked up the fence unit and began to lug it around the side of the house. It was awkward, and none too clean, but she persevered, finally depositing it on the porch at the back door.

'Is he married?' Karen asked idly, dropping her suitcase a sensible distance away.

'No.'

A wide smile curved her cousin's pretty mouth. 'Well, imagine that! I think I'm going to enjoy this holiday. Unless he's your project of the year?' At Camilla's horrified look, Karen smiled like a sleepy kitten. 'Why not, Cam? He's gorgeous. Still, I can't say I'm sorry. If you had him in your sights I'd have to lay off.'

'Dave didn't like him.' It was offered as a reason for her lack of interest.

The arched brows lifted even more. 'Why?'

Camilla shrugged. Her cousin gave her a sharp look, but went on lightly, 'Well, if you're not interested, that gives me free rein. I can hardly wait!'

When Camilla arrived back from the evening milking, she found Karen seated on a chair in the shabby little dining-cum-living-room listening to the radio.

'I see you still haven't done any redecoration,' she commented wryly, getting up to turn the set off. 'I know Dave didn't like spending money, but there should be more than two comfortable chairs in the house! Why don't you get a television set?'

'No money,' Camilla replied laconically. 'I'll go and have a shower before I start dinner.'

'Don't hurry, I've already organised it. I guessed you were planning to have the cold meat in the fridge, so I made a shepherd's pie and some coleslaw and a pudding.'

Which touched Camilla. Normally she ate cold meat and salad until the joint was gone, and then roasted another, and so began the whole process over again. After her shower, in honour of the occasion she pulled on a dress, one from her trousseau. Its blues and mauves were flattering, as was the deep neckline and narrow waist.

'Very nice.' Karen eyed her with appreciation when she walked into the sitting-room. 'For an Amazon, you have a surprisingly fragile air. Too fragile, by the looks of you. You need feeding up. I assumed you wouldn't have anything to drink so I bought a bottle of wine. There's yours, on the table.' Waiting until Camilla had sat down, she lifted her glass. 'Cheers. Here's to a pleasant winter.'

Camilla gave her a startled look. 'Are you planning to stay that long?'

Karen laughed, but quickly sobered. Her voice was even, almost hard as she answered. 'I don't know. I'm sick of Auckland. I've lost my job.'

Camilla stared. 'What happened?'

'It's a long and none too edifying story. I fell for the boyfriend of the owner, not realising who he was. He dumped her, she found out why and dumped me, and then he decided he wanted her back again.' She directed a blind smile at Camilla, not trying to hide her chagrin and pain. 'We were planning to go to Tahiti today for three weeks. Last night he rang and told me it was all off, so I split. If I like it here I might stay, if I can get a job, and you can bear to have me. You don't know of any boutique owners who want a trustworthy saleswoman, do you?'

'No, but there are a couple of shops in Bowden that certainly could do with someone to liven them up. And you know you don't have to ask, I'd like nothing better than to have you here.'

Karen drank some of the wine. 'We could try it,' she said casually. 'If we end up hating each other's guts, we'll part amicably. Well, here's to the future.'

Camilla found herself wondering in a rather depressed way just what her future held for her. She felt—old, as though the feast of life was passing her by before she had more than tasted a few crumbs.

It was almost dark outside. The breeze had dropped and the sky was a clear, warm yellow. Somewhere in the distance a cow lowed; closer to hand crickets wound their shrill little instruments. Through the open window came the thick, overpoweringly exotic perfume of datura flowers. The white trumpets glimmered in the dimness against the dark hedge. A blackbird sang with heartbreaking beauty. It was Camilla's favourite time of day, yet behind her appreciation was a deep restlessness that shadowed her responses. She lifted her glass and drank to the toast.

'Why didn't Dave like Quinn?' Karen probed, her voice lazily curious.

Camilla shrugged. 'He rubbed Dave the wrong way right from the start,' she began carefully.

'That wasn't hard to do,' her cousin observed with amused frankness.

'That's not——' She subsided under the older woman's direct gaze. 'Well, all right, so Dave could be difficult. Quinn wanted to buy the place even before we moved up here. His lawyer's letter arrived about two days after the one that told me Uncle Philip had died.'

'Why does he want it? Sorry, love, but it's no great shakes as a property, is it? I know it was Dave's dream come true; in fact, if he hadn't wanted it so much you wouldn't have kept it, would you? When you told us that you were going to marry him and live here, we were astounded. He'd always been just the boy next door. We didn't even know that you were in love!'

Camilla's shoulders stiffened. In a light tone she said, 'I wanted to come up here, too.'

Karen drank some more wine. 'If you say so,' she said in her brutally honest way. 'But why did the handsome and oh, so worldly Quinn Fraser want to buy it? That homestead looks as though it's surrounded by thousands of fertile Fraser acres. Why should he want more?'

Camilla sighed. 'This place is an enclave, surrounded almost entirely by Falls station. The road ends here, and even that belongs to Falls; it's a private road. Apparently one of Quinn's ancestors gave the block to someone who had saved his life. He was supposed to give it back when he died, but he sold it instead.' Loyalty to both her uncle and Dave kept her silent about the other reason Quinn had for wanting to buy them out.

'Ah, I see. So you're smack in the middle of the Fraser acreage. I thought he looked a very territorial creature. Well, now I know why your delicious neighbour wanted to buy the place, but I'm still in the dark as to why Dave and he were at daggers drawn, apart from the fact that Quinn is everything Dave would have liked to be.'

Camilla made a small sound of protest, but Karen fixed her with a steady regard. 'You know he was damned prickly and possessive; he didn't even like the fact that we were close friends as well as cousins.'

Because Dave had been insecure, and for an excellent reason. Her eyes suddenly filling with tears, Camilla said harshly, 'My uncle hated Quinn for some reason, and said so in a letter that came with the will, so Dave came up ready to dislike him. When we got here there was a dispute about the boundary fence and the water rights. We take our water from a dam on Quinn's property, and Quinn said that the rights died with Uncle Philip. Then our bull got through the fence on to his place, and he shot it. Dave was furious—rightly so, I think—but Quinn paid him the animal's value.'

'And Dave was even more furious,' Karen guessed shrewdly, 'but he took the money.'

'Yes.'

'Poor old Dave. He made life hellishly difficult for himself—and you, too, by the sound of it.'

Camilla made no attempt to deny it, but she couldn't bring herself to agree, either.

'Has Quinn been at you about water rights and things? Since Dave died, I mean.'

'No.' Camilla picked up her wine-glass. 'He gave up on that shortly after we got here. He rang to say he'd come up with a way of renegotiating the whole thing, and after he went overseas his lawyer dealt with it all. But the episode didn't make for good neighbourly relations.'

'No, it wouldn't,' Karen agreed drily. 'His absence must have made things easier for you. I wonder why such a gorgeous man hasn't been snaffled up? I gather he does like women?'

The question roughened Camilla's nerves. Angry with herself, she looked into the clear golden depths of her wine. 'Oh, he likes them. Beautiful, rich ones. As you can imagine, the gossip-go-round has a wonderful time, but he doesn't flaunt his love-affairs.'

'I wonder if he'd be interested in a good-looking poor one?' Karen mused, then gave her delicious chuckle. 'I must say, he's the most exciting creature I've come across. That superb self-confidence! There's something about a man like that—you can't help wondering what it would be like to be the woman who makes him lose his cool completely.' She smiled cynically. 'Of course, they usually don't. They've had women panting after them almost from the cradle and they're far too conscious of their own value! He might have been discreet, but I bet he's had enough experience to be a wonderful lover. You can always tell, can't you?'

A strange white-hot shudder shot through Camilla's body, so unnerving her that she forgot to breathe. Startled by an image of Quinn Fraser, lean and dark and powerful, bending over the white body of a woman in bed, she took a large mouthful of wine in an effort to banish it. The cool liquid ran, tangy yet sweet, down the back of her throat, helping to settle her stomach back into its proper place.

She had never before visualised Quinn as a lover. It occurred to her now that she had been very careful not to. Karen's assessment of him was no doubt accurate. She had never made any secret of her own experience; probably it helped her recognise the same quality in others. Camilla, who had made love with only one man in her life, didn't know, and didn't want to.

Raggedly she said, 'I'd better go and check the dinner.'

In the small, inconvenient kitchen she stood looking vacantly around. Ignoring the soft simmering of the saucepans on the stove, she put her hands on the bench and pressed down, lost in a wave of primitive human need, the hunger for a body close to hers, a voice to talk to in the dark. For the space of a few seconds, she allowed every urge and desire in her rebellious body to surge free, making her unbearably aware of her loneliness and the needs that she kept so firmly repressed.

Slowly her will reasserted itself. The raw hunger ebbed, leaving her cold and frightened by the intensity of the experience. It had to be simple self-pity. And the undertone of sexual appraisal in Karen's voice when she spoke of Quinn. Her frankness had reminded Camilla of all that she now missed. That was all. So, justifying and minimising the emotion, she tried to forget it by dishing up the dinner.

After they had eaten, they spent the evening finishing the bottle of wine as they caught up with each other's lives, and retired early, although not perhaps early enough for someone who had to be out of bed at five to milk cows.

Camilla went to sleep with a lighter heart than she had had for months. The prospect of having Karen stay was pleasant. Living in the same street all their childhood, they had been always been friends in spite of their very different personalities. The older by three years, Karen embraced the freedoms of modern life with enthusiasm, while the circumstances of Camilla's life had precluded any such experimentation, but they had remained close.

After breakfast the next day Camilla garnered up a pair of gardening gloves and said casually, 'I'll see you at three this afternoon.'

'Where are you going?'

'I work for a market gardener just down the road.' She pulled a face. 'Cutting broccoli this week!'

Karen gave her a dismayed look. 'How often do you go there?'

'Four days a week, whenever Joe wants me.' There was no complaint in her voice. Although the work was hard and left her exhausted, she needed the money.

That evening Mrs Fraser rang up. 'We've just heard that a couple of Members of Parliament are doing a tour of the north, and they're staying the night here. Quinn feels that they should hear from as many farmers as possible exactly how their policies are affecting us. Do say you'll come, dear, with your cousin,' she coaxed. 'Buffet dinner, and there might be dancing for you younger ones if you want it. We don't want to be too obvious about things!'

Quashing her instinctive refusal, Camilla looked across at Karen's lovely, expectant face, and weakly agreed.

'Fast worker, isn't he?' Karen said, smiling at her thoughts. 'What shall I wear?'

'Something pretty, but not too formal.' Camilla was frowning, mentally reviewing her wardrobe with the dismal conviction that there was nothing in it at all suitable except for her blue and mauve dress. The same dress she had worn to almost every other social function since she had arrived in Bowden.

'I think I have just the thing,' Karen gave a slow, languorous smile. 'Are you going to be dressing up for anyone in particular?'

Camilla got up and went into the kitchen to put the kettle on. 'No. I—it's too soon.'

Karen waited until she had bought the tea-tray into the room before saying calmly, 'Dave's death was an appalling shock, a tragedy, but he wouldn't have wanted you to mourn him for the rest of your life.' She eyed Camilla up and down. 'And widowhood is no excuse for being a frump. You need a decent haircut, and those hands look awful. Believe me, I know women who'd kill for legs like yours, and what do you do? Hide them under baggy old jeans!'

Camilla set the milk-jug down with a small crash. 'I don't have the money,' she said, tight-lipped.

'What do you mean?'

'Just that. The farm barely brings in enough to cover the interest on the mortgage. I live on what I make working in the market garden. I have no money to spend on clothes or make-up or haircuts.'

Karen leaned forward, her face astonished. 'Wait a moment. If you can't make the place pay—why are you still here?'

'Because no one wants to buy a place that's too small for anything other than goats. The bottom has dropped out of the property market.' She smiled mirthlessly. 'There's a recession on, Karen.'

'Can't you sell to Quinn? He doesn't look as though he's suffering from any recession.'

Camilla recalled long legs in superbly cut trousers, a fine Italian shirt and a jacket that had been put together by a master tailor. 'He's different,' she said, ruthlessly dragging her mind away. 'The Frasers are old money. They started out in the last century, and haven't looked back. He chooses to live here, but he has interests all over the world.'

'A millionaire!'

Camilla's smile was oddly lop-sided. 'He doesn't splash it around, but yes, I suppose he must be. Anyway, I don't think he wants to buy the farm any more. He hasn't said anything about it.' Since the last time she had turned him down, six months ago.

Karen looked really intrigued, her eyes sparkling with interest. 'Not a yuppie, share-market millionaire, either. I met enough of their women in the boutique: arrogant as hell, dripping with ostentatious jewellery, flipping across to Sydney to buy their clothes. I must say I was rather pleased when the stock-market crashed, even though it didn't do the boutique any good. Well, well, well!'

Feeling distinctly edgy, Camilla drank her tea, starting a little when Karen emerged from her pleasant reverie to ask, 'What are you doing tomorrow? Does your market gardener need you?'

'No.' She smiled with faint irony. 'I'm going to set up the electric fence and try it out. I'll check the cows and the in-calf heifers, and in between get some work done in the shed. It needs tidying before winter.'

'I can't see myself being of much use to you there, so I'll do the housework.'

Camilla looked around with a grimace and a faint sigh. 'I'd love it if you did. I don't get much time——'

'None at all, if this is how busy you're kept. And don't thank me, I like doing it.'

Which was true. For all her sophistication, Karen had always been the more domesticated of the two. Camilla gave her a grateful smile. 'Things will be easier when the cows are dry. Milking night and morning is a tie.'

'The whole business seems a drag to me,' Karen said frankly. 'Especially as it's for nothing.'

When she went out after breakfast the next morning, Camilla was inclined to agree with her. It was sunny, but dark clouds against the hills to the west warned of rain to come, and the wind was cold. Camilla pulled her old oilskin a little closer and strode off towards the tractor shed with Ben loping along beside her. The clouds emphasised the green of the paddocks to an intensity that was startling. Still, it was now cool enough not to have to worry about facial eczema, which was a relief.

Once she was on the tractor, her spirits lifted. She manoeuvred it carefully across the culvert between the house and the cowshed, and on down the rutted race between the paddocks towards the farthest field, her eyes searching the landscape in a fashion that had become a habit now. When she reached her destination she began to whistle as she turned the engine off and jumped down.

She hammered in the thin iron standards for the fence, then organised the business end, nodding with satisfaction as the power surged through with a satisfying series of clicks. From now on, any cow that reached too far for another succulent clump of clover was going to get a good, sharp jolt! Smiling, she loaded the spare bits and pieces back on to the tray. She stepped up, sat into the hard iron seat, and turned the key.

The starter motor whirred then screamed, and a sudden, terrifying puff of smoke gushed out, but there was no response from the engine. Sick with fear, because she couldn't carry on without the tractor, she turned the key off and flung herself to the ground. Her hands shook as she yanked up the bonnet, muttering words that would have horrified her mother. Of necessity she had become an amateur mechanic, but the tractor was old and the prospect of a bill for repairs made her stomach tighten. Her nostrils quivered at the strong smell of smoke, and the icy panic in her midriff intensified.

'Having trouble?' a voice drawled from behind her.

She whirled around to meet Quinn's green gaze. Her heart performed a complicated manoeuvre, and, pushing her hair back from her eyes, she said shortly, 'Yes, the wretched thing won't go.'

'Checked the plugs?'

'First thing.' Exasperation sharpened her tone. His presence was easily explained, for tied to the fence was his horse, a big grey. He must have been riding the boundary and come upon her while her head was deep in the entrails of the tractor. But Ben should have barked.

She glared reproachfully at the dog, only to find that he was wagging a traitorous tail while his lip lifted in the peculiar grin that she had thought to be her particular prerogative.

'Have you any idea what the trouble could be?' Quinn's voice was deliberately, provocatively patient.

'No. I just turned the key on and the starter motor made an appalling screech and there was a gush of smoke.'

'And the main motor didn't fire?'

'Not a chug,' she said tiredly.

'Do you mind if I have a look?'

'Be my guest.' Her flippant answer masked chagrin, and fear. If the tractor failed it would be impossible for her to carry on.

He leaned into the engine, his hands moving deftly among the various parts, apparently not upset by the fact that they were becoming marked by oil and dirt. Camilla stood silently, wondering why the sight of those hands should affect her in such a strange way. She felt a heated melting in the pit of her stomach and slivers of ice down her backbone.

He straightened, catching her eyes on him, and said, 'I'll see if I can get it going now.'

But the starter motor made the same dreadful noise, and he turned it off immediately, looking down at her with comprehension. 'There's your problem. I'm afraid the bearings in the starter motor are shot.'

She bit her lip. 'I see.' Almost, she asked him how expensive it was likely to be to fix, just catching herself up in time. Straightening her shoulders, she finished composedly, 'Thank you. I'll get the garage to send someone up to look at it.'

He proffered a handkerchief. 'Clean this morning,' he said, smiling rather sardonically down at her.

Meekly she cleaned as much of the dirt from her own hands as she could before handing it back. He did the same, then said, 'You have a patch on your forehead. I'll see if I can find a clean spot—ah, yes.'

He was standing too close, yet she didn't step away as her instincts insisted. Instead she waited with her breath imprisoned in her throat while he moved the cloth across her forehead. When his hand stilled, his eyes dropped to meet her wide, startled stare and she thought she could read some sort of satisfaction in their dense green depths.

For a stretched moment they stood close, then he stepped back, saying prosaically, 'It's not exactly clean, but better than it was,' as he stuffed the handkerchief back into the pocket of his moleskin trousers.

Camilla hurt as though she had been kicked over the heart. Fortunately Ben came ambling up, so she stooped to pat him, and when she straightened up again her colour was once more normal.

But it was a very shaken woman who walked back with Quinn across the paddock, stroked the persistent nose of his big grey, and watched as he rode away with his relaxed stockman's seat, completely at one with the animal.

Karen was sympathetic, but she didn't realise what a blow it was. When Camilla rang the tractor people they said they'd send someone up to have a look at it that afternoon. Morosely she drank her morning tea, commented distractedly on the flowers Karen had arranged on the table, and went out again, wondering if the bank manager would be approachable and knowing full well that he wouldn't be.

On the way she deposited a bucket full of kitchen scraps with the pig, scratching his back for a few minutes as he rooted happily among the potato peelings. His sack of pellets, guaranteed to turn him into a sleek and happy animal, had just about run out. More expense. The power bill was due, and she was expecting a bill from her insurance company. During the six weeks before calving in late July she would have very little income except for the bonus cheque, all of which was already earmarked for essentials, and what she could earn in the market gardens.

Desperation darkened her thoughts. She felt so tired— she was almost always exhausted—and she had no idea how to go about pulling herself out of the mire. Perhaps she would feel fitter when she no longer had to milk twice a day, but winter brought its own duties.

Oh, Dave, she thought. We were so young, you and I. Eighteen and twenty-two. I thought I loved you so much; was it just because Mum had died and I was alone and you were my first boyfriend? Hormones and loneliness. And were you so possessive because deep down you realised that I didn't love you as you deserved to be loved?

By lunchtime she had had to cover the tractor engine with a tarpaulin. The weather had closed in and it was raining steadily. She wondered whether she should try to tow it into the shed, but decided that if she asked her elderly car to do such a thing it would probably die on her too, just for spite.

She spent a depressing afternoon doing the books. Karen ironed some of the clothes that Camilla had been tossing into a pile in the spare bedroom for months, then washed her hair and curled up by the fire with one of the selection of fashion magazines she had produced from her bag.

'Here,' she said, holding out a page as Camilla went through, 'this would look good on you. You've got the looks to carry it off. Unusual—no, *exotic*. You're not in the least pretty, but you stand out in a crowd.'

Camilla surveyed the fantastic creation, and the equally fantastic model beneath it, and snorted. 'So would someone with two heads. Ancient jeans suit me better.'

'You're hung up on the conventional!'

Laughing, Camilla retorted, 'So is everyone else. That's why there are conventions!'

The shrill summons of the telephone silenced them. It was Quinn, his deep tones cool and deliberate. 'Dean

Sanderson will be down shortly to tow your tractor inside. I presume you want it to go to the machinery shed?'

For a moment she could do no more than goggle at the sun-drenched scene that decorated the calendar on the wall.

With impatience colouring the words, he asked, 'Is that where you want it to go?'

'Well—yes, but you don't have to——'

'I know,' he interrupted, amusement not far below the surface. 'It's my good deed for the day. Equivalent to helping two little old ladies across a busy road.'

An unwilling bubble of laughter choked down the hot words that sprang to her lips. Taking this for assent, he continued, 'He'll be down in ten minutes or so. Goodbye.'

After staring blankly for a moment at the silent receiver, Camilla finally hung it up, two emotions warring within her. One was relief. The other was a slow, dangerous resentment, all the stronger for not being voiced.

But beneath and a part of them, as yet almost unrecognised but more potent by far, was fear. Quinn could sap her strength by coaxing her to rely on his. It would be so easy to lean on him, to slip back into the habit of letting someone else take the lead and make the decisions.

Dave's death had been a useless tragedy, but it had brought out hitherto unused strengths and qualities from her. She would not—could not—allow her new-found independence to be wrested from her. It was a matter of survival.

'Who was that?'

Karen's question startled her. 'Oh—Quinn. He's sending someone across to tow the tractor into the shed. The garage mechanic won't be out in this weather.'

'That's kind of him.'

She nodded. 'Yes. A neighbourly thing to do.' She snapped out of her mood to give a twisted smile. 'Big on chivalry, is Quinn. Comes of being an only child, I suppose. If he'd had sisters he might be a little less protective.'

Karen chuckled. 'I can't see it. He looks as though he's as possessive as hell, as well as chivalrous and a little arrogant. All the macho attributes. Ah, well, I'm always prepared to sink my feminist principles in a good cause. Or for a good man.'

Through the sound of the rain beating on the iron roof came the heavier, deeper thrum of some piece of machinery. Shortly the Falls' big tractor came to a grumbling halt outside the house. Camilla saw the movement of an arm in the cab as the driver waved, and she set off for the back porch. A few minutes later, clad in oilskins and leggings, she ran towards the tractor, rather enjoying the stinging drops on her face beneath the hood. Her long legs moved easily as she climbed into the cab and grinned at Dean.

'Lovely day,' he said as he put the enormous and expensive behemoth that was his pride and joy into motion.

'You wouldn't notice a hurricane in this thing. Windscreen wipers! On a tractor! And a tape deck! Whatever is the world coming to?'

He laughed. 'Ah, the days are gone when tractor drivers had to sit it out in all weathers. Quinn makes sure that his workers get only the best.'

He enlivened their trip down the race with a hymn of praise for both the tractor and his employer, pausing only to peer down at the narrow width of the track across the culvert. 'I don't like the look of this. One good rain and the whole lot would wash away. You'd better get a bulldozer in to fix it, or you'll wake up one morning and find that you can't reach the cowshed.'

Camilla knew. Knew, too, that she had no way of doing anything about the culvert until she'd managed to rake up some more money. Aloud, she said, 'It's under control.'

He gave her a shrewd glance. 'If I tell Quinn——'

'No!'

'OK,' he said peaceably, but he was frowning.

Worry drummed away in her mind as they came in sight of her stranded tractor, forlornly abandoned in the middle of the wet green paddock. It abated a little when they had manoeuvred the thing back to the shed.

Once inside Dean climbed down and said, 'Well, Camilla, let's have a look at this. The boss says she's blown her bearings.'

It took only a moment to convince him that 'the boss's' diagnosis was right. 'Yep, that's it. You know, I've got a contact who could get them up to me in no time at all. What say I give him a ring? They'll come on the bus and I can put them in for you the next day. It'll cost you a lot less, and save you time. I know the garage is pretty busy this time of year.'

'I can't let you do that.' But, oh, how she wished she could. 'Quinn pays you to look after his machinery, not mine! It's very kind——'

'Don't you worry about that. I'll do it in the evening.' He grinned widely. 'Lisa and I are saving up for a baby— I hear they come expensive now, and we've only got seven months to get there! The extra money will come in handy, believe me.'

He named a sum that made Camilla bite her lip, but even so it was less than she had feared, and, if Karen got a job and shared some expenses, she might, with the most rigorous economy, be able to afford it. When the cows were dry she could work full time at the market garden.

'You're sure Quinn won't mind?' she asked tentatively.

'I guarantee he won't.' He looked a little self-conscious, but went on, 'How can he? It's in my own time.'

She allowed herself to be persuaded. 'Thank you, Dean. I'll be eternally grateful. How lovely for you that you're going to have a baby! Tell Lisa I'm very envious, won't you? How is she?'

'Blooming! Well, I'll contact my man, and give you a ring as soon as I've finished the job, will I?'

'Yes. Thanks, Dean.' She hesitated, then said again, 'You're sure it will be all right with Quinn?'

'Certain,' he said, in such a positive voice that she was convinced. 'He's no slave-driver, though he expects his due, so I'd better stop gossiping. Don't worry about the old tractor, she'll be good as new.'

'Thank you,' she said, with a sudden, flashing smile that made him boggle slightly.

She walked back to the house, allowing the delicious feeling of relief to steal over her. It was a setback, but one that she could overcome. If it occurred to her that the tractor was still old, as was all the vital equipment on the place, and her budget stretched to its limit now, she suppressed the thought. Back at the house she told Karen of Dean's offer.

Shrewdly, her cousin asked, 'Can you afford to pay him?'

'Yes. Just. But I hope to heaven nothing else gives up the ghost.'

'It was kind of Quinn to send him across. I suppose he hoped Dean would offer to do it.'

'Quinn?' For some reason Camilla didn't want Quinn to have anything to do with Dean's offer. Shortly she retorted, 'He's not kind. Neighbourly, perhaps, but he has the reputation of being ruthless in his personal life.'

'That doesn't worry me. I'm not exactly the soul of ruth, either,' Karen assured her flippantly. 'How ruthless?'

Camilla was sorry that she had been goaded into the indiscretion. 'It's just gossip, nothing definite. I shouldn't have said anything.'

CHAPTER THREE

LATER, with the throb and hiss of the milking machine as background, Camilla recalled an incident that had happened when she had been married only a few months. She had come across a woman who was sitting on a log in the patch of bush down by the creek. Tears had swollen her lovely eyes, but she was over the worst of her paroxysm of weeping when Camilla came upon her and stopped, startled and concerned.

'Sorry, did I stray over the fence?' the woman asked in a low husky voice.

'Well, yes, but it's all right, you're not in the bull paddock.'

The woman produced a laugh. It took some effort and it was painful, and Camilla gave her full marks for effort. 'At the moment I couldn't care less. Any old bull would be welcome to me.'

Camilla said awkwardly, 'I doubt if you'd think so with one breathing down your neck.'

'No, I suppose not. The will to survive is strong even when all seems lost.' Her smile was a stiff movement of pale lips. 'Oh, well, I suppose you know what it's like. No, actually you look too secure and satisfied for anything so traumatic to have happened to you.'

Camilla couldn't hide her bewilderment and the woman elaborated with wry insouciance, 'Being jilted. Well, no, that's not quite right. He's just given me the push. It's the first time for me, and I'm afraid the stiff upper lip needs practice. It serves me right. Usually it's me who does the dumping. I hope that I've never hurt anyone quite as much as this.' She blew her nose and wiped her eyes with a scrap of handkerchief. 'Up until now I've always believed that a tactful farewell eases the pain. I've just discovered that it doesn't.'

By now Camilla knew who she was. Several times she had seen her in the car with Quinn. Tentatively she asked, 'Would you like to come up to the house and wash your face?'

'That bad, is it? OK, bless you.' But she made no attempt to get up. 'I know who you are, now. The thorn in Quinn's side. I hope you and your man just stick in there—the bastard—no, that's not true. It's not his fault I started seeing wedding bells. Or hearing them. I mean, it wasn't as if I hadn't been warned. But he's so bloody gorgeous, we just fell over each other to offer ourselves up for the next sacrifice. He never makes any promises, and he's such a fantastic lover...'

She was so gallant in spite of her pain. After a wash and a swift repair job to her beautiful face she had drunk a cup of tea and gone, leaving Camilla full of sympathy and profoundly thankful that she had never had to suffer such a blow. By contrast, her own courtship had been pragmatic and steady; no great heights, she thought, thankful for it then, but no depths, either. Neither she nor Dave was made of the stuff of passionate lovers.

And if occasionally she had suspected that perhaps the ecstatic heights made the pain worth bearing, she had repressed such subversive thoughts very firmly.

She wondered now whether Karen would be able to cope with Quinn. Of course, he might not be interested. But Karen was truly beautiful, with a wilful, provocative loveliness that had attracted the eyes of men since she was fourteen. And, of course, she would know how to deal with him. She had had a string of admirers ever since she was old enough to know the value of her secret, seductive smile, and she had known exactly how to manage every one.

Except that none of them had been Quinn Fraser. Camilla recalled the direct green glance and the tough line of jaw and chin, the intangible yet potent air of masculine competence, and wondered ironically whether any woman would ever be able to *manage* Quinn Fraser.

It was odd; when she allowed her imagination free reign she could picture him—somehow now only too vividly—as a lover, his handsome face drawn by passion. But when it came to visualising him in love, the severely angular features softened by tenderness, she couldn't do it.

Behind the enigmatic mask lay—what? Certainly not an ordinary man, but in what ways extraordinary she had little idea. All that she knew about him was what he allowed others to see: the sexual charisma, potent and unforced, the air of authority, the charm, and the subtle warning, unconsciously conveyed by voice and gesture and glance, that it would be dangerous to anger him.

She had seen him angry on the day he'd shot their bull, and she had never been so frightened in all her life. Yet when Dave had died he had been incredibly kind, the latent harshness that had intimidated her temporarily softened. Kind—yet detached. So what sort of man was he?

The sort of man it was wise to steer clear of, she told herself flippantly as she hosed the bails down in the thickening darkness.

The three years since she had been there had not dimmed Camilla's memories of the Falls homestead. Keenly alive to beauty, she had admired the house, but remembered it best for the warm welcome she had found there. And her surprise when later Dave had said that

he found the house stiffly formal and the owners cold
and 'snooty'.

Now, as she sipped sherry while looking around what
could only be called a drawing-room, she responded
again to that indefinable welcome.

It suits the Frasers, she thought, her glance passing
from the tall figure of their host to his mother, also tall,
and very fashionable in an understated way, her greying
hair gleaming in the light of the lamps. It was difficult
to imagine Mrs Fraser at home in a starkly modern
setting. The Georgian-styled wooden panelling made a
splendid background for her upright carriage and chiselled features. Mother and son shared those features,
but what was refined and feminine in the mother had
become subtly transmuted to an intense masculine virility
and strength in Quinn.

Camilla's eyes came to rest on him as he smiled down
at a laughing Karen. Always intimidated by his splendid
physical presence, she had only lately allowed herself to
analyse its impact, noting the contrast of dark chestnut
hair and olive skin with the brilliant Celtic eyes, as green
and transparent as an emerald. Camilla envied him those
eyes because her own were so pale, a translucent grey
that seemed washed out behind her black lashes. In
photographs she looked as though there was nobody
there. Even the deep violet of her dress, abetted by the
matching colour Karen had applied to her eyes, couldn't
lend more than a touch of fugitive colour to them.

But it was not Quinn's looks nor the lean power and
grace of his body that made him so blatantly attractive.
What impinged immediately on any woman was the aura
of male sexuality combined with a bone-deep, understated power based on character and intelligence.

It was certainly registering with Karen. And very
potent it was, if the barely subdued glitter in her sherry-
coloured eyes was anything to go by. The rising note of
excitement in her voice made it more obvious, as did the
flush beneath the expertly applied make-up.

It seemed indecent to watch this—and in some strange
way it hurt. Camilla dragged her eyes away, but not
before they were snagged on Quinn's stare. He was
watching her watching Karen, and in his eyes there was
something that drove the colour from Camilla's skin.
She gave him a small, tense smile, and he responded
before shifting his gaze back to Karen. But Camilla had
the strangest feeling that, although he was looking down
into her cousin's vivacious face, his attention was still
on her. She sucked in her breath, fighting a weird empty
feeling in her midriff.

Someone in a group claimed her attention and she
turned away thankfully, using their undemanding
company as a barrier. Slowly she began to relax, even
to enjoy herself, an enjoyment that dissipated like drizzle
on a summer road when she found herself alone with
her host.

Camilla was immediately on the defensive. He was
looking at her with an oblique smile which was not reflected in his eyes. After a strangely tense moment he
said softly, 'This is the first time I've seen you fully made-
up. One of the first things I noticed about you was how
very red your lips are. That and the fact that your eyes
are far too slanted to be as innocent as your smile, and
that they are the clear, pale colour of the sky at dawn.
So transparent, so cool, and yet so impossible to read.'

Thank heavens Karen had insisted she wear foundation, because with any luck it might tone down the
colour that swept her face. She said hastily, 'I can't see

how the slant of my eyes—or my smile—has anything to do with innocence.'

'Perhaps not. Allow me my fantasies.' There was the hint of a taunt in his voice.

She didn't know if it was reflected in his eyes because she didn't dare look up. Instead her gaze skittered around the room, finally coming to rest on Karen, at her ease and sparkling up at a group of clearly dazzled men, among whom, she noted, was the local veterinarian, John McLean.

'She's perfectly happy,' he said blandly. 'Are you cold? Come closer to the fire.'

Her skin was prickling, but not from the cold. Because she couldn't think of anything sensible to say, she allowed him to take her over to the carved fireplace.

She blundered into the silence by saying inanely, 'This is a very gracious room.'

'Falls has been lucky in its owners. They loved old things, but built to the most up-to-date standards of their time, and always with an eye to saving work. So many Victorian houses relied on an army of servants to function properly, and they are now impossible to look after.'

'You sound very—impersonal—about your fore-bears.' She met the cool enquiry of his gaze with a slight movement of her shoulders, as though she were trying to ease into too tight a garment.

'I don't go in for ancestor worship. I'm grateful be-cause most of them had the insight to avoid excesses, and I respect their sterling qualities. However, mankind can't be viewed in the same light as stock. With people, breeding is unimportant compared to character and upbringing.'

His unblinking regard pierced her. Her lashes drooped as she raised her glass to her lips, using it as a shield against that subtle violation.

Another pause, one she rushed to fill with more too rapid words. 'I must thank Dean for doing the tractor. It goes like a charm, and he didn't charge me very much for it at all. It saved me quite a bit of time. When I rang the garage they said that they wouldn't be able to do it for a week or so. I'm sure that trundling things around in the wheelbarrow would do wonders for my figure, but I wasn't looking forward to it.'

'Your figure is good enough. You don't need to work out with a wheelbarrow,' he said calmly.

Camilla blushed like a schoolgirl, cursing herself for her lack of poise. He didn't sound as though he was complimenting her; the tone of his voice indicated merely that he was making an observation. And 'good enough' was hardly enthusiastic. Her glance collided with his. He was unsmiling, only the slight narrowing of his eyes revealing that he was aware of her embarrassment.

Grabbing for some sort of self-possession, she managed to say evenly, 'Thank you. It shows what hard work and clean living can do.'

'You have good bones,' he said, his appearance of indifference belied by a warm, smooth undernote in his tones. 'Like a racehorse, slender and graceful, with surprising stamina. Why does a simple observation of fact startle you so much? Surely it's not the first time anyone's told you that you look like a thoroughbred?'

'Well, actually, yes,' she owned, frankness overcoming her embarrassment. 'As for compliments from you, you must admit I have a right to be flustered.'

'My irritation with Dave,' he said tightly, 'did not extend to you.'

'Yes, it did.' Her voice was very steady, as steady as her glance.

He was looking down at her, a muscle clenching beside the hard line of his mouth. Almost as if he forced himself to relax, the tiny flicking died away and he resumed the mask, smooth and implacable.

'Understand this,' he said without emphasis. 'Dave began it, possibly because of Philip's one-sided feud. I didn't respond until it became obvious that he was prepared to use the same tactics as your uncle: straying stock, refusing to mend boundary fences, being as obstructive as possible. Neighbours in the country need to work together, not be at loggerheads. Unfortunately Dave used me to work off his insecurity and feelings of inferiority. I was prepared to give him time; however, he wasn't prepared to yield any ground.'

Awkwardly, because he was right, she said, 'He wasn't normally like that. He could be difficult, but usually he was much more reasonable. I don't know why he was so——'

'Bloody-minded,' he supplied.

'You were just as bad! Totally unreasonable!' Then, because she was essentially a just person, 'To begin with, anyway. Insisting that the water rights died with Uncle Philip. And you didn't have to shoot the bull.'

'No.' His brows drew together as he drained the last drop of sherry from his glass. After a moment he said, 'I have a quick temper. And I probably wouldn't have shot the damned bull if it had been the first time it had happened. But it was dangerous. Remember when I had to help you put it back in the paddock, the time it got on to the road and bailed up the school bus? It was the last straw. It put you in danger. Your uncle had refused to get rid of it and so did Dave, even when I offered to buy him a new one that wouldn't stray and was less ad-

dicted to school buses. That was why I shot the bloody
thing—that, and the fact that when I did it was in the
throes of charging me.'

She went white, appalled at the image of him in
danger. Then she said slowly, 'I—I find that hard to
believe. Dave would have told me.'

'Why?' He held her eyes, his own direct and merciless.

'Well—why shouldn't he? What did he have to gain
from keeping it quiet? We were partners—we discussed
everything...' But her voice trailed away.

'Everything?' Quinn asked softly. 'Dave was essentially a loner. He did what he wanted, made his own
decisions without any pretence at consulting you.'

Fortunately Karen came across then, trying but failing
to hide the inquisitive gleam in her eyes, and Camilla
was able to escape to the safety of another group. In the
ensuing conversation she tried to forget the lazily
caressing note in Quinn's voice as he'd enumerated her
physical characteristics.

With only partial success. The trouble was that to him
that sort of thing was a game. He was accustomed to
seeing women as objects to be admired solely for their
beauty. Dave's strength had not lain in open appreciation. An occasional 'You look nice' had been his limit.

She was horrified to find out how vulnerable she was
to a drawled compliment, a slow, appreciative scan of
her body. The problem was that she was inexperienced
where men were concerned. At school her unusual face
and her height had kept boys away. Naturally they had
been attracted to bright, pretty girls like Karen. Dave
had been her first love, her only lover.

Quinn's remarks made her wonder now whether she
had known her husband at all. 'Essentially a loner...'
In a way they had been very familiar strangers. A lifetime
of living next door to each other had meant very little

when there were four years between them in age. Even when they had fallen in love, Dave had found it difficult to express his feelings. She had been so eager for it to be true, to become close to someone, that she had not thought beyond the immediate fact of his loving her... It had been selfish of her...

Guilt of a particularly potent sort ate at her, guilt that she tried to ease by talking cheerfully to all she met, ignoring the fact that her eyes kept flicking across to find Quinn as he made his way about the room, urbane, sophisticated, completely at home with everyone.

Shaken, Camilla applied herself to being the perfect guest and forgetting her host. She didn't manage it, but the effort kept her mind under control.

Dinner was superb: crayfish and avocado salad and delicious lamb, with vegetables so fresh that they could only have come from the station garden, served with excellent New Zealand wines. To follow there was a fantasy of puddings, delicate concoctions of subtropical fruits as well as a New Zealand invention, the pavlova, an edifice of meringue and whipped cream decorated with lime-green slices of kiwifruit. Camilla stayed with Karen and John McLean, aware that Quinn and the two Members of Parliament were just behind them, Quinn's head tilted as he listened courteously to something one of the MPs was saying.

Conversation hummed about them, until Karen asked brightly, pitching her voice a little, 'Why is this place called Falls?'

Quinn turned, smiling at her with amused indulgence. 'Up in the hills behind us,' he told her, 'there's a waterfall on a tributary of the river that runs through Bowden. It's about a hundred feet high, and the first settler here called the land he bought after it.'

Karen flashed her vivid smile, asking, 'Is there any chance of mounting an expedition to see it? Could I find my way there by following the river up from the bridge, or would that create havoc among your animals?'

'We'll organise a trip before you go home,' Quinn promised.

'Oh, super.' Karen almost purred.

Camilla was disgusted by a pang of envy. Life seemed so simple for the Karens of this world. She would thoroughly enjoy her trip to the waterfall, and if Quinn made love to her she would enjoy that too, and when it was over she would shrug as she had done with her other lovers and go on her way with only kind thoughts of him. Why should she be so uncomplicated, whereas for Camilla everything was so difficult?

She had never seen the falls; Dave's prickly pride had seen to that. More guilt churned within. It seemed shameful that she should be eating Quinn's food and drinking his wine, so acutely conscious of him that she thought she could see him with her skin, when both her uncle and her husband had refused to accept his hospitality.

His voice, lowered and somehow too intimate, made her start. 'You're looking very pensive. Something worrying you?'

'No, not at all.' Aware that Karen's attention was half on John, who was talking earnestly to her, and half on them, she summoned an airy smile and tried to infuse a casual note into her words. 'To tell the truth, I was wondering what the weather was going to do.'

'According to the latest report, Australia has sent us a high which is moving slowly enough to give us three or four days of fine weather with crisp nights. Have you ever noticed that when people say "to tell the truth," they invariably lie?'

Camilla's eyes flew to meet his. They were coolly sardonic. She pressed her lips together before saying in an off-hand voice, 'Really? How perceptive of you.'

'When you evade a question,' he went on remorselessly, 'your lashes flutter for a moment, as if you have to make a real effort to do it. Don't ever try to lie, will you? You'd give the game away immediately.'

'What it is to be so astute!' she marvelled, disturbed again at the personal note of the conversation. She made the mistake of fixing him with what was supposed to be an insolent stare, but it was doomed, for he smiled at her, a teasing, warm, completely understanding movement of his finely moulded mouth, and she stopped thinking. Her heart began thumping unevenly in her ears and she was assailed by a strange tingling sensation in every nerve.

He said softly, 'Do you want me to tell you how you look now, Camilla?'

Karen's voice as she claimed his attention once more had never been so welcome. Gladly Camilla stepped away. When Quinn smiled at her like that it would pay to keep in mind the fact that he wanted the farm. Enough, perhaps, to use his undoubted masculine expertise to flirt a little with her, as he had been that evening. Perhaps he too thought that widows were so desperate for love that they could be persuaded into indiscretions by the offer of a little warmth, a little sexual flash.

Well, she was not so hungry for masculine attention that she could be seduced into parting with the property. According to Philip's will, if she did sell to Quinn she would lose all her rights to both the land and the money made in the sale. If that happened, she would not be able to pay off the bank. She simply could not afford to do it.

After dinner more people arrived to meet the guests, and there was dancing. Just after Camilla saw Karen in John McLean's arms she caught sight of Mrs Sorrell, Guy's mother, and enjoyed a chat with her until the older woman looked up with a smile on her face.

'Hello, Quinn. You're just in time to take Camilla off and dance with her,' she said heartily.

Camilla began to protest, but a swift glance into Quinn's face told her that there would be no escape. Trying hard to look as though dancing with him was going to be a pleasure instead of a penance, she allowed him to lead her into the ballroom and went stiffly into his arms.

'Relax.' His voice was amused. 'You didn't try to imitate an iron standard when you were dancing with Guy.'

She drew a deep breath and relaxed. And because she was a born dancer, a creature of grace when music played, after a few moments the magic worked on her and she allowed her instinctive sense of harmony to take over.

'You dance beautifully,' he said after a few seconds.

She smiled. 'So do you.'

Because the tune was a slow sentimental ballad most of the dancers had welcomed the opportunity to embrace each other and were drifting about the room, closely intertwined. In a painful heightening of her senses Camilla felt his hand at her waist, firm yet not demanding, his other holding hers in the same impersonal grip. He was wearing a dinner-jacket that had been fitted by a master tailor, and the white shirt emphasised his dark attraction and strong angular features. He smelt faintly of something pleasantly astringent, and beneath that was his own masculine scent, warm and earthy and immensely alluring.

Camilla's body reacted with a slow stirring, the sexual appraisal that marked the onset of desire. Without volition her gaze crept upwards, lingering on the ruthless beauty of his jawline and the stark, well-cut symmetry of his mouth. A muscle pulled beside it, and her eyes lingered on the tiny betrayal, then lifted, slowly, and were helplessly, hopelessly enmeshed by his. Narrowed beneath half-closed lids, glinting with an emotion that she didn't recognise, they were very hard.

The unspoken communication between them was stark and as fierce as lightning. He smiled without humour and his grip tightened, pulling her to rest against him in an embrace that sent warning signals racing through her.

Dazed, Camilla clenched her teeth on to her bottom lip. He was too experienced not to be aware of her vulnerability, so he was deliberately tantalising her. From a myriad of pressure points each tiny nerve-ending sent a message of pleasure and anticipation to her brain. Yet she couldn't pull away, because her mind, too, was in thrall to the potent pull of his virility.

Nervously her tongue touched suddenly dry lips. As if she had signalled to him, his eyes blazed with crystalline fire. A faint dew sprang out across her temples and she turned her head away, staring with unfocused gaze across the room.

She said vaguely, 'This is a lovely party.'

'Yes.' His voice sounded oddly strained, but when he continued he spoke in his normal deep, relaxed tones, free from the urgent undercurrent that she had heard before. 'I thought it was high time MPs learned how their agricultural policies are affecting us. I notice they're listening to a variety of complaints, and from the occasional pained expression that slips through the political mask I gather that they're not liking what they hear.'

It was a relief to follow his lead and embark on a political discussion. After the tape stopped and he escorted her back to the drawing-room, she even managed to delude herself into thinking that what had occurred in his arms had been a temporary aberration.

But it came back to haunt her later when she lay in her lonely bed and felt again the heart-stopping sensations that he had roused in her so effortlessly, with such mocking ease. And at last she admitted that she had never known what it was like to desire a man. The caresses she had known from Dave seemed perfunctory, a casual fulfilling of an inconvenient need.

She had been so innocent. Her mother had told her little of the dynamics between man and wife; her father had died so soon after their marriage that when her mother referred to him it was with wistful sentimentality, as of a long-ago romantic affair, so Camilla had known nothing about sensuality.

Dave had begun gently, but too soon for her his awkward tenderness had become fierce and uncontrolled, so that his embraces had been almost an ordeal. Now, looking back, she thought that he had probably been as inexperienced as she had. Either that, or his desire had made him careless of the fact that she needed preparation and care to be able to enjoy lovemaking. It added to her guilt that she had been unable to give him what he'd needed from her. She wondered if that was why he had turned to the farm as a means of working off his frustrations.

Nothing in her marriage had prepared her for the primitive impulses that coursed through her body whenever she was in Quinn's arms. He felt it too; her face heated in the friendly darkness as she recalled the flickering fire in his eyes. She thought of the contrast of his dark golden skin against the milky pallor of hers, and visualised an enormous bed with dark, silken sheets and the scent of jonquils, Quinn bending over her, her fearless acceptance of his fierce regard... Her mind drifted, wicked with imaginings until, blushing, she banished the erotic pictures from her brain.

Such indulgence was dangerous. To counteract it she thought of how easy it would be for him to woo the title deeds of the farm from her through a sensuous haze, and then for her to find herself like the woman she had befriended when they had first come to the farm, weeping with grief because he had taken what he wanted and had no further use for her.

Camilla was horrified to discover jealousy at the memory of the dance her cousin had shared with Quinn, and the laughter and conversation she hadn't been able to ignore. Talking to John McLean at the time, she had noticed that he, too, was keeping an eye on the couple. She hoped he wasn't going to be hurt by Karen's light-heartedly cynical attitude towards love and relationships.

The evening had left a sour taste in Camilla's mouth—so much so that she went to strenuous lengths to avoid thinking of it. Fortunately the following day was fine, one of those magnificent autumn days when the russet chrysanthemums flamed in the garden beneath a sky of mellow blue, which was cloudless and serene, and the barely perceptible breeze brought with it the scent of grass and the fresh perfume of the patch of bush that sheltered the home garden. Camilla mowed the lawn, and after lunch went down to work in the market garden. By the time she got ready for milking she was so tired that her bones ached.

'Why do you have to work at the weekend?' Karen had spent the afternoon on a chair on the front porch, soaking up the sun. 'You make me feel like a slug.'

'You're on holiday!'

Karen frowned. 'It's you who needs the holiday, not me. You always were fine-drawn, but you're looking positively scraggy now.'

'Thanks a million.' Her eyes wandered over the saucy little shorts and sun-top that her cousin wore, and she asked impulsively, 'Do you feel better about the fiasco in Auckland?'

Karen's smooth shoulders lifted in a moody shrug. 'Oddly enough, I think I do. You're sensible, Cam, you've never allowed yourself to get into the kinds of messes I do. And although I'd have enjoyed Tahiti, I don't know that it would have been any more fun than meeting Quinn.'

'I see.' Camilla looked hesitantly at her cousin, but she was reading again, her face smooth, so Camilla went slowly into the wash-house to pull on her milking clothes. Sophisticated and experienced though she was, Karen did not know much about men if she thought that Quinn would be fun! He was subtle and complex, and hard to read because he took good care that no one got too close to him.

And how do you know that? Camilla scoffed. You know nothing about the man, except that he is unscrupulous and admits to a bad temper, and he has an odd effect on you, an unpleasant appeal that you'd better kill before it has a chance to develop into some sort of weird obsession.

Firmly forbidding her mind to dwell on him, she went off to the shed. However, when she arrived back at the house, cold and tired, Karen met her at the door, bubbling with pleasure. 'Quinn rang. He wondered if we'd like to see the local production of *Finian's Rainbow*, so I said yes, and he's calling for us at seven-thirty.'

Camilla could have wept. 'I really don't feel like going out tonight,' she said, gesturing at her splattered overalls and boots.

'Nonsense. I've run you a bath; you'll have time to soak for twenty minutes and wash your hair, and you can use my drier. It won't take long to eat dinner—I've made mutton stew and vegetables, with cheese and fruit to follow. If we keep moving, we'll even have time for a cup of coffee.'

Camilla tried again. 'The local production of *Finian's Ranbow* doesn't seem like your thing.'

'Quinn Fraser is my thing.'

Camilla had to smile. 'And I suppose if I say I'm tired, you'll——'

'Tell you you're stagnating, and refuse to go myself. You need to go out. Brooding at home like a hermit is not good for you.'

Her voice was very firm, but Camilla could read the real concern and care in her expression. After a silent moment she gave a rueful smile. 'No, I suppose you're right. OK, let me at the bath.'

She wore a dress that had been new when she'd married Dave. It had not been one of her more inspired choices, and was out of date now, but it was warm and the deep green suited her, she decided, as she put on lipstick and a touch of blusher that was the same vintage as the dress.

Once she had not minded never getting anything new, but—oh, perhaps it was just Karen's arrival, with her fashionable clothes and sleek chic. Camilla thought that just once she would like to be able to go into town and spend a hundred dollars frivolously. She had never been extravagant. Money had been a worry all her childhood, becoming even tighter when her mother had developed the illness that was to kill her. There had been nothing to spare for fripperies, not then, not when she and Dave had come to the farm. She hadn't minded; she had been as eager as he to build up their equity in the land.

When had it come to seem less worth while? When had her emotions become apparent for what they were: the need for some human warmth in her life? Oddly enough, she could remember the exact day that her uneasy concern about her emotions had crystallised into a sure knowledge. It was when she and Quinn had herded the belligerent bull back into its paddock, using Ben and one of the Falls dogs to work together as a team.

Somehow, for no reason, it had been a turning-point. In fact, if she closed her eyes, she could recall each incident, as clear and vivid as though it were engraved on her mind.

Wincing, she banished the burning little pictures from her brain. It was then that she had realised that she was fond of Dave, she liked and admired him, but she did not love him. She had been trapped by love, trapped by circumstances, and for a time she had panicked.

A cynical little smile curled her mouth. Karen had said that she was not in the habit of making a mess of her life, but Camilla had known then that she had done exactly that, and she had wanted nothing more than to run away.

Of course, she hadn't gone. She had promised to love Dave and honour him, and if she couldn't do one, she could at least make sure that he never knew of it.

However, she had needed time to become accustomed to her new understanding of herself. That had been one of the reasons why she had refused to have a baby. There had been others, ones that should have made sense to him. With Dave working full time for a contractor, she had been needed to run the farm. If she had had children so soon, she knew that they would have been locked into a cycle of under-captalisation and near poverty all their lives. But he, normally so hard-headed, had persisted with his demand that she become pregnant until she'd been forced to say no outright.

It had hurt to refuse him. After he'd been killed she'd wondered if he'd had a presentiment and wanted something to fling in the face of the fate he sensed, a part of him left behind to thwart the will of whatever jealous gods had ordained his death. She had denied him, and now she was going to spend the evening in the company of the man he had resented so bitterly.

'Ready?' Karen appeared at the doorway of the bathroom. 'You know, you look good when you make up. I know Dave had a thing about "painting your face", but you should wear cosmetics. Apart from anything else, skin as pale and as fine as yours is very prone to skin cancer. At the very least you should use a sun-screen all the time.'

'I do,' Camilla said, straight-faced. 'A hat.'

'That old knitted thing? It should have a brim.' She stopped, cocked her head and smiled, her eyes sparkling. 'That sounds like the man. See, I told you you'd have time to get ready!'

CHAPTER FOUR

OUTSIDE it was cold, but the sky was sprinkled with enormous stars, four planets in close conjunction making a splendid sight to the north-east.

Karen exclaimed, and Quinn, a tall outline in the darkness, pointed out each one. 'Venus is the brightest, known as the evening star. The reddish one is Mars. Saturn is yellowish, and the largest is Jupiter. It's a rare sight to see them all together.'

'I'll always remember it,' Karen said extravagantly as he put her into the car.

He came around to open the door for Camilla; with his fingers on the handle, but the door still closed, he asked quietly, 'Will you always remember it? This is the first occasion we've been out together.'

Her mouth dropped slightly, but before she had time to answer he had the door open and she slid into the back beside Mrs Fraser.

Camilla was determined to enjoy the show. The local company was fortunate in possessing a reservoir of good male and female vocalists, enough of whom were also competent actors, and enthusiasm and a really professional wardrobe mistress compensated for any lack of polish. Camilla knew and liked the songs and, in spite of the nagging reproach that seemed to have taken up permanent residence in her chest, she was ready to be pleased.

Which she was, although she hadn't enjoyed the eyes that had watched them come into the War Memorial Hall. It was kindly curiosity, but it made her shrink a little. And she would rather not have found herself sitting next to Quinn. But as soon as the lights went down and the curtain went up she was lost in the adventures and misadventures of Finian McLonergan, his daughter and the leprechaun Og in some mythical part of the Deep South.

When interval arrived they all went into the supper-room for coffee and biscuits; Camilla introduced Karen to all who came up, and listened in on a considerable amount of gossip.

On the few occasions that she and Dave had gone out everyone had been friendly, if a little reserved. Bowden was an old-established area and it took a while for the locals to accept newcomers. But as guests of the Frasers their reception was quite different! Some looked surprised—at least until they saw Karen—but all were more than coolly friendly; the occasional person was almost effusive. Karen sparkled, enjoying herself immensely. She looked very lovely in a cowl-necked dress of bouclé knit, its autumn tones enhancing the tawny lights in her hair and eyes. Beside her Camilla felt awkward and frumpish.

And full of self-pity. She wished wistfully that she were four inches shorter and didn't look such a nonentity, with her high cheekbones and colourless eyes and skin. What would it be like to be so confident of a welcome, so arrogantly, self-possessed as Karen was—and Quinn?

'Penny for them.'

Startled, she looked up, parrying the cool enquiry of Quinn's glance with a protective gleam of irony. 'I was wishing that I were small and pretty and outgoing.'

His brows lifted in somewhat mocking surprise as he surveyed, at leisure and with narrowed gaze, every inch of her length. When he had finished she was pink-cheeked and her eyes were glittering like affronted jewels.

His tone was sardonic. 'Why? I prefer subtlety. You
are just the right height for—conversation.'

He smiled teasingly as the colour glowed through her
skin. He had been going to say for kissing, she knew it!

Blandly, he continued, 'You know, anyone watching
us would think that I have just made an improper
suggestion, one that surprises you, but to which you're
not entirely averse.'

A harassed glance revealed that no one else was
listening to this outrageous conversation. Frostily, she
retorted, 'Your imagination is working overtime. No one
could possibly think...' She floundered, wondering how
to rescue herself, and was saved by an imposing woman
across the room who smiled at her, then deliberately at
Quinn. 'There's a woman over there trying to catch your
attention,' she said thankfully. 'A large woman in a
purple dress——'

'I don't know her,' he countered, not even looking.
'Why does it embarrass you when I compliment you?'

'If you think I'm going to answer questions like that
in the middle of this crowd, you must be mad. Anyway,'
she added, far too late, 'I'm not embarrassed.'

Her temper, normally placid and hard to rouse, was
definitely bubbling. Casting another hunted look around,
she smiled weakly at the openly curious woman in purple,
and wished with quite unreasonable fervour that Karen
would stop talking to Mrs Fraser and John McLean and
intervene before she found herself indulging in a verbal
free-for-all with the totally infuriating man who was
smiling down at her with a hard edge of mockery.

'Pull the other leg,' he said maddeningly. 'But not
now. Interval's over.'

Breathing deeply, she swept back into the hall. She
even swapped seats with Karen, not caring how pointed
it looked. But he had successfully spoiled the evening

for her. The magic of suspended belief would not be recalled. Something else to be set down to his account, she thought angrily, dragging her wayward gaze away from his strikingly angular profile and back to the stage.

Sunk in thought, she barely heard the conversation in the car going home, rousing only when the vehicle turned in through the great trees at Falls instead of carrying on to the end of the road. It appeared that Mrs Fraser had invited them in for a nightcap. Camilla took in a deep breath but it was too late to object, and, besides, Karen was obviously delighted. Very sternly, Camilla girded up her loins to be polite but not effusive to the man who helped her so courteously out of the car. It didn't help that she could sense his amusement all the way into the house.

Consequently, when Quinn paid her only the barest minimum of attention, reserving his smiles and most of his attention for Karen, she should have been pleased, if not relieved. It was therefore infuriatingly inconsistent to feel a smouldering anger at both of them, bolstered by a loneliness so deep that it appalled her.

Before she finally sank into exhausted sleep that night, Camilla found herself trying to summon memories of Dave, of their lovemaking, but she found it impossible to recall how she had felt. Slow tears oozed from beneath her lashes. Unable to afford a honeymoon, they had come straight to the farm, and Dave the lover, the husband, had almost immediately been superseded by Dave the farmer. He had worked with a driven fervour that exhausted him so that most evenings he was too tired to do more than fall into bed and sleep.

It had been a pattern that continued. She, too, had been exhausted each night, and the moments of passion had been rare, and, 'Face it,' she told herself fiercely, brutally, 'unsatisfying.'

Perhaps Karen, with her unabashed attitude towards love and sex, had the right idea: enjoy life as much as possible with no commitment and no recriminations. For Dave the farm had been all-important. Since childhood he had yearned to work his own land with a hunger that left little place for anything else. Recognising that a farmer must be dedicated to survive, Camilla had accepted with what now seemed surprising complacence the rapid evolution of their marriage into little more than a business partnership.

I was happy, she protested silently, vehemently. But how had she measured her happiness; against what? Guilt tugged at her with its choking fingers. She knew why she was lying here in the bed she had shared with Dave thinking of their love-life together, and the reason was in all probability sleeping soundly in his bedroom at Falls, not half a mile away.

Admit it, she sneered angrily, soundlessly, you want him. Even to herself she wouldn't say his name, because that would mean the acceptance of far more than she was prepared to admit.

Bewildered and shocked, she went out into the kitchen and poured herself a glass of water. The liquid cooled her dry throat, but did nothing for her mental turmoil. Back in the bedroom a soft wind puffed the thin curtains into the room. She stood motionless for long moments at the window, staring out across the garden and the paddocks beyond. A pukeko called from down by the creek, a harsh cry so familiar that she barely noticed it. The beautiful blue-black swamp hens, with their scarlet legs and beaks and their amusing habit of flipping a white tail as an alarm, usually made her chuckle, except when they were infuriating her with raids on her garden.

The intense flood of moonlight picked out individual trees in the bush that sheltered the house from the cold southerlies, laying beads of silver along branch and leaf. Ben's chain rattled as he stretched outside his kennel and looked towards her. Nothing escaped Ben; as well as being an excellent cattle dog, he was a good watchdog.

Camilla felt the old awe, the deep, atavistic restlessness that a clear night roused in her, a yearning part emotional, part spiritual. Her soul swelled and expanded, and a profound longing for she knew not what ached in her heart. She craved to discover the riddle of the universe. A bitter little smile curved her lips. The universe indeed! she scoffed soundlessly as she made her way back to the bed. You don't even understand yourself!

Almost certainly it was tiredness that made her silent and morose at the breakfast table.

'Oh, you poor old thing,' Karen sighed. 'Two late nights in a row is obviously too much for you. I should have let you go to bed last night. Now, me, I feel fantastic!'

She looked fantastic, too: clear-eyed, bubbling with health and excitement. Hiding a yawn, Camilla poured another cup of tea in eloquent silence.

'I like the vet,' Karen said, making a face at her cup. 'Pass me the milk, will you?'

'John McLean? Yes, he's a nice chap.'

'Single?'

Camilla shrugged. 'Divorced. Local rumour hath it that his wife was a bitch of the first order.'

'I'd like to hear her side of the story.' Karen's voice was very dry. Peering into her cup to make sure that the generous helping of milk had changed it to a colour she was more comfortable with, she remarked airily, 'He seems rather smitten with you. Spent quite some time telling Mrs Fraser and me how good you are with animals.'

Camilla was astonished. 'He might think that, but I can assure you he's not smitten.'

'Why do you automatically back off when any man shows interest in you?' Karen swallowed a tiny amount of tea, and looked across the table as though she had made up her mind. 'You'll probably hate me for saying this, but honestly, Cam, it's for your own good. I can't bear to see you wearing yourself to a thread because you feel some sort of obligation to Dave's memory. God knows, this is no life for you. You should be out enjoying yourself at nights, not hurrying home because you have to get up at the crack of dawn to milk a herd of cows!'

Camilla said carefully, 'If you'd wanted to stay later, you only had to say.'

'No, I don't mean that!' She gestured at the table and the room, both shabby and old, and then at Camilla's much-washed sweatshirt and faded jeans. 'You've got great blue circles under your eyes and you look ten years older than you are. Why don't you sell the place and find yourself a job you like doing?'

Camilla drained her tea before saying defensively, 'I like being my own boss, I like the life. I feel—fulfilled here.'

'But?' Karen said astutely. 'What's the but, Cam?'

'But the place is not big enough.' Camilla looked out of the window, her lashes drooping. 'Don't repeat this, but this year I'm going to be hard put to it to make enough to service the debt. If I don't, well, I'll have to sell.'

Resting her chin on her hands, Karen surveyed the downcast face on the other side of the table. 'But if you can't make a living from it, would anyone buy it?'

'That,' Camilla said evenly, 'is the crunch. As a hobby farm, perhaps. The bottom's dropped out of the property market, and with the share-market collapse there's no likelihood of anyone buying it for an investment.'

'So the obvious person to approach is Quinn.'

Camilla hesitated, before muttering, 'I can't sell to him.'

'Why? Because Dave didn't like him? Don't be silly, Cam. This is not a matter of loyalty! If I read you right, you could be facing a bankruptcy sale! He's filthy rich. He wouldn't have any trouble finding the money.'

'It's not that easy.' Camilla picked at a thread on the tablecloth, working the thin cotton back and forth. After a moment she looked across at her cousin. 'Uncle Philip only left it to me on condition that I didn't sell to Quinn.'

Karen's face was a study in astonishment. 'Why would he do that?'

'I don't know. All I know is that he hated Quinn, and stated in his will that if I sold to him the money was to go to charity. All of it. So I wouldn't be able to pay off the bank. And yes, that would mean bankruptcy.'

'Strewth!' Karen was astounded, her golden-brown eyes snapping with emotion.

'It gets worse,' Camilla told her miserably. 'When Dave was dying he made me promise again.'

'*Dave* did?'

'I don't know why. Most of what happened between them was Dave's fault. Quinn was incredibly rude to him—to you he's all charm, but when he's angry his tongue is cruel enough to flay skin. And he was often angry with Dave.'

'Dave wouldn't like that,' Karen stated. 'He hated to be in the wrong, didn't he?' Then, 'What on earth did Quinn say to him?'

Camilla shrugged. 'I don't know. He wouldn't bawl Dave out in front of me.'

'He has got nice manners. Emphasised by the distinct probability that he could forget them in moments of great passion. Hints of leashed violence excitingly close to the surface, and more than a touch of ruthlessness in that splendidly sculptured jawline.' Karen's grin was irrepressible, but it faded almost immediately. 'Your uncle must have been a miserable old toad! Why did he do it? What are you going to do?'

Camilla stood up. 'Why? I don't really know. As for what to do, I'm going to stay here for as long as I can.'

Karen looked at her with some surprise. 'You sound quite passionate! More passionate than I've ever seen you, I think. Why don't you think about getting married again? That'd fix——'

'I'm not getting married just for the sake of solving a problem!'

'I suppose you want romance with a big R?'

Camilla smiled rather ironically. 'I don't know that it exists.'

'Oh, it exists all right, but not, I'm afraid, in marriage. Or not for long, anyway. Marriage is for wear and convenience and the procreation of children, not for romance and glamour. If you want that, go in for affairs.'

Camilla's smile matched the cynicism of Karen's observation. 'I haven't got the time.'

'No, you haven't.' Karen cocked her head as a roar from the road announced the arrival of the milk tanker. 'That thing certainly makes a row.' She watched the great silver truck cross the paddock towards the cowshed, slowing down as it went over the culvert. 'How do you keep the milk fresh until he comes?'

'Come over to the cowshed and I'll show you.'

Surprisingly, Karen took her up on it. After breakfast she walked out across the paddock and went through the shed, listening carefully as Camilla explained the whole process from the time the cows moved into the bails to the final departure of the milk in the tanker.

Looking about her at the huge stainless steel vat that chilled the milk, she observed, 'This must have cost a packet. The mortgage?' At Camilla's nod she grimaced. 'And now the interest rates are astronomical...'

'Yes. It was fine while Dave was alive, he made big money contracting and we could service the loan, but now—oh, well, it's done.'

Karen nodded briskly. 'Does Quinn have a dairy farm?'

'Several, but not here. There are some Perendale sheep on Falls, but Northland is marginal for sheep. What we do really well is cattle. Quinn breeds Charolais Hereford crosses for beef, and he has a Hereford stud that his father started. He exports Herefords as far away as America.'

Karen looked impressed. 'All that and dairy farms too? He must be loaded.'

'He heads a sort of family corporation that deals in primary produce, all sorts—orchards, freezing works, deer farms—you name it, the Frasers have a finger in the pie.'

'Then why does he live here? You'd think that Auckland would be far more central.'

Camilla shrugged and said dismissively, 'I suppose he thinks of Falls as home. And nowadays, with electronic wizardry and planes, he doesn't have to live close to all the action.'

'I suppose not. Why do you think he's got to what—thirty, thirty-one—without being married? It's not his looks or his manners.' She rolled her eyes and growled tigerishly. 'He's stunning, and he's well aware of his own appeal, so why is he still playing the field?'

Camilla gave a funny little grimace. 'Perhaps he prefers it. He might share your ideas about marriage. You might be able to get away with asking him that sort of question, but I find him damned intimidating.'

'Yet you stand up to him,' Karen observed.

Her cousin's penetrating survey made her shrug and give a small smile. 'If I didn't, he'd take over. Beneath the veneer of chivalry he has bulldozer instincts.'

Karen turned away. 'Chivalry? I wonder.' She was still for a moment, before her lovely laugh accompanied an elaborate shudder. 'Definitely hidden depths. I wouldn't like to cross him, but it's that element of danger that adds so immensely to his appeal.'

Made uncomfortable by the open appreciation in her tone, Camilla somewhat clumsily changed the subject, relieved when her cousin followed her lead. They went for a walk around the farm, arriving back at lunchtime just as a large black cloud began to creep across the sky.

'It looks,' Camilla commented with resignation, 'as though the weather forecast was a little out of kilter.'

Sure enough, it was raining by the time she went to get the cows in, and the rain continued with some force all through the night, ending in a torrential downpour while she was milking the following morning.

On the way back to the house she heard the roar of the flooded creek with dismay, stopping with a sharp intake of breath at the culvert. On the house side of the creek the roadway was completely washed away, exposing one side of the large concrete pipe. The water that raced so eagerly through the gap had carried off the metal that formed the track, leaving the big foundation stones scattered like marbles down the creek bed.

She and Ben were able to scramble across, but there was no hope of the milk tanker getting through. Almost weeping at the thought of the money it was going to cost her to get the crossing repaired, she hunched her shoulders against the drizzle and walked back to the house. She had decided not to approach the bank manager about the tractor; by using the strictest economy she would be able to make up the shortfall, but this latest disaster meant that she would have to beard Mr George in his den. If he refused... But she would face that when—*if* it happened.

As she scratched behind Ben's wet woolly ears before tying him up, she thought wearily that even the fates seemed determined to get her off the farm. Whatever happened, she was going to have to reopen the roadway, for if the milk tanker couldn't get through the following day she would be in real trouble.

Once inside, she rang the quarry. The woman in the office promised that the metal would arrive either that afternoon or the next morning. Her soft mouth held under tight control, Camilla put the receiver down and went over to the desk to pull out her last bank statement. The figures were engraved in her brain, but she looked again, just in case she had somehow overlooked anything that might help her deal with this latest catastrophe without seeing the bank manager.

Karen emerged, frowning as Camilla explained what had happened. 'I see,' she said slowly. 'How much is it likely to cost?'

With a fierce gesture Camilla flung the paper down. 'I don't know. A truckload of metal doesn't come cheap.'

'Will a truckload of metal do it?' Karen asked shrewdly. 'Won't you need a bulldozer too?'

'No, I can use the tractor to do the heavy stuff.'

She didn't say that she had helped Dave with it the last time, or that it would probably only last a couple of years this time, too. It needed a concrete framework to hold the metal so that the force of the flood couldn't scour it away. Instead she was going to have to replace the foundation stones and then dump the metal on top, and keep her fingers crossed.

'You will not!' Karen was scandalised. 'Those stones are far too big for you to be trying to move. Quinn——'

'No.'

Only one word, but it stopped Karen in her tracks. 'All right,' she said slowly. 'You're working at the gardens again today, aren't you? Come and have your breakfast. Nothing will seem so bad after you've had something to eat and a charge of caffeine.'

It wasn't true, but after a valiant effort Camilla managed to eat an egg and a piece of toast.

The truck arrived just as she turned into the gateway after her stint in the gardens. The driver stopped outside the house, swinging down from the cab as Camilla let an impatient Ben off his chain.

'Where do you want the stuff, lady?' he asked. He was young, good-looking in a hard-bitten way, with an overbold stare that made Camilla feel that her jeans were too tight and her shirt had one button too few done up.

'Straight ahead down the drive. The culvert over the creek has washed out.' She stifled her dislike under an air of brisk efficiency.

'OK. Want a lift down?' The offensive survey he conducted of her body negated any possibility of kindness.

'No, thank you.' Her voice was cool and dismissive.

'OK, lady, you're the boss.'

Lighting a cigarette, he climbed back into the cab, leaving Camilla a little uneasy. Another chauvinist who thought that widows were fair game. How she hated that easy, degrading assumption that she needed a man so badly she would go to bed with anyone who offered!

Fuming, she strode off to move the in-calf heifers into a new paddock, then shifted the electric fence so that the milking animals would have fresh grass for the night.

By the time he had dumped the load she was on her way back to the house to change for milking. She checked the work, and found it well done. Somewhat calmer, she told him so when he presented her with the time-slip. Of course, he took her few words of praise as encouragement.

'I'm good at what I do,' he drawled, the words heavy with innuendo.

Ignoring him, she concentrated on the slip, noting that he had filled in the times correctly.

'Here, sign it.' He proffered a ballpoint pen.

Hurriedly she signed, handed both the paper and the pen back and stepped back, saying, 'Thank you.'

He was in no hurry to go. Flashy, sure of himself, he grinned at her. 'Big job you've got there. You need a man about the place, Mrs Evans. I could give you some help.'

'I can manage,' she said icily.

He laughed softly and put his hand on her shoulder, his fingers tightening when she tried to wrench herself free. Catching her wrist with the other hand, he pulled it against his chest, his fingers digging deep into her skin.

'See, you're not very strong at all,' he drawled, his pleasure at her helplessness written plain in his features.

A cold fury gripped her. It gave her the self-possession to stand quite still. Through clenched teeth she said, 'You are just about to lose your job.'

'Only your word against mine, lady.' But he loosened his grip a fraction.

Holding his insolent gaze with her own, she said quietly, 'The quarry can't afford to lose the custom, believe me.'

He laughed unbelievingly. 'Your custom? Come off it, Mrs Evans. This is all the metal you've ever got from the place, and it wouldn't pay my wages for a week.' His voice thickened as his eyes lingered hotly on the soft swell of her breasts. 'You just relax and be nice to me, and I'll see that you don't have to worry about lonely nights any more. You must be ready for a man by now.'

'Get the hell out of here!' Taking him by surprise, she kicked his shin, dragging her hand away as she twisted sharply towards him, her shoulder and elbow buffeting him hard and painfully in the chest before she jumped back.

Swearing, he lunged at her, his face red and sweating. But Ben was between them, the hairs along his back bristling with fury as his lip lifted in a snarl made terrifying by the growls that reverberated from his throat.

'Call him off!'

Camilla grabbed the dog's collar, only just restraining him.

'No, Ben, *no*!' She hauled back with all her might. He obeyed, but his hackles and his growls proclaimed his intention to attack the man whom he kept in his gaze with paralysing intensity.

She said quietly, 'If you ever set foot on this place again I'll charge you with trespass and assault, and see that you lose your job.'

'You haven't got that sort of pull,' he retorted, his meaty hands clenched by his side, but well back out of Ben's reach. 'Like I said, lady, it would be your word against mine. And everyone knows what widows are like. Who'd believe you?'

He was grinning cockily, and she realised that he really did think that he was perfectly safe, that he could do what he liked and get away with it. For a moment her mind was blank, but inspiration followed. 'Quinn Fraser, for one,' she said calmly. 'He'd believe me.'

Her words wiped the smile from his face. 'Oh, I see,' he sneered, turning away with a shrug. 'Sleeping with the upper classes, are you? Well, lady, if I'd known whose property I was trespassing on I'd have driven straight past, believe me. Give me a ring when he's had enough of you.'

As a parting shot it couldn't have been bettered, his knowing leer tarnishing her relief at his departure. He even managed to swagger as he walked towards the truck, although she spoiled his petty triumph by letting Ben go, an action the dog took as permission to attack, so that the driver had to run the last few steps.

After the sound of the engine had died away and Ben had been rewarded with a dog biscuit, Camilla found that she was shaking, one hand unconsciously massaging the wrist that had been maltreated while her face burned with anger and humiliation.

As she attended to milking the cows she mulled over what had happened. Common sense told her that she was not to blame, that the whole sordid incident had been the driver's fault, but she couldn't stop herself from wondering dismally if there was something about her that provoked such familiarity.

Although Quinn was much more subtle, was he really any different from the man who had just left? He wanted her land, not her body, and to acquire it he was prepared to flirt. Hardly honourable. She had, she thought ruthlessly, been physically repelled by the driver, but fairness obliged her to admit that she was not by Quinn. On the contrary, she was fighting a very strong attraction, one she hated to acknowledge.

Physically, of course, he was all that a woman could ask for in a man. Superb good looks based on a splen-

didly moulded bone structure, all the authority that
height could give, and that poised, lithe athlete's body.
He walked with the smooth grace of a predator; he
exuded the virile charisma of a sexually successful male.
And, to go with all that, he had a sharp intelligence and
a masterful character, effortlessly, unconsciously
dominating with his air of masculine competence.

And she was exposed to all this without any sort of
defence. He had the power to make the years with Dave
seem pedestrian and untouched by magic. As perhaps,
she admitted with immense reluctance, they had been.

She bent to slide the cups on to one of her favourites,
stopping for a moment to pat the warm brown flank.
Outside the sun had gone down in a glory of gold and
tangerine, and the swift dusk was overlying the hills,
turning the sky from porcelain-blue to a grey the colour
of a dove's wing.

As she went about mechanically cleaning up and
tidying away, her mind went around and around, dis-
secting her marriage. Old ground, and with it came the
nagging, unbearable guilt, because Dave had loved her.

It had taken Karen, with her clear, dispassionate
understanding of Dave's character, and Quinn, who had
refused to allow her to fool herself any longer, to make
her see the truth. It was possibly this realisation that
made her careless as she hosed the yard down, so that
she drenched herself thoroughly, and once back in the
washhouse had to strip to her underwear.

'You're looking glum again,' Karen said commiser-
atingly when she came in. 'Are you still worrying about
that wretched crossing? I wish I could offer you a loan,
but I'm as near broke as makes no difference. I spent
all my savings on wonderful clothes to wear in Tahiti!'

'No! I'll see the bank manager.' She gave a wry, heartbreaking little smile. 'Heaven knows, compared to the

amount I already owe him this will be peanuts. Anyway, I should be happy. The cows are giving so little milk that from tomorrow I'm going to milk them only once a day.'

'Really? What happens then?'

'I'll dry them off at the beginning of May. Then I have a quiet time until July. Then they calve, which is when all hell will break out.'

Karen had been stirring soup. Her gaze focused sharply on Camilla's shoulder and she put the spoon down. 'What happened?' Camilla's hand went up to cover the bruises and Karen added pointedly, 'On your wrist, too. Who's the he-man?'

The words filled her mouth with acid. 'The driver of the quarry truck.'

Karen looked at her sideways. 'Do you know him?'

'I've seen him around occasionally.'

Karen's mouth closed with a snap. 'The bastard! Are you all right? Why didn't you scream?'

'I set Ben on him instead and threatened him with losing his job. He didn't try anything more.'

'What made him think that you'd be interested in a roll in the hay?'

Camilla shrugged. 'All the world and his wife knows that widows are so eager for a man, they're ready for sex any time. Didn't you know?'

The other woman's breath hissed out between her lips. 'No,' she said slowly, 'I didn't. Do you have much trouble like that?'

'No. Oh, they look, sometimes they make heavy innuendoes, but usually that's all. I can freeze off anyone who might get over-eager.'

'The nerve of them! Will you complain to his employer?'

Camilla shook her head. 'As the man said, it's only my word against his.'

'But he might come back!'

'No. He's not stupid. He knows that he won't get away with anything again.'

'Well, if you say so.' Karen's doubt was obvious. 'I think you should complain. After all, if he's prepared to come over caveman with you, he might well try it on others.'

'I'm the only young widow about.' Camilla went through into her bedroom. She had no intention of revealing that she had threatened the driver with Quinn, or the construction he had put on her words. The last thing she wanted was for it to reach Quinn's ears. In fact, the mere thought of that happening made her cringe as she showered and hastily got into a skirt and shirt.

But Karen returned to the subject after dinner, urging anxiously, 'Cam, how can you be sure that creep won't turn nasty and lie in wait for you?'

'No. He knows that I wouldn't hesitate to have him up if he did make a nuisance of himself. Don't worry, I can take care of myself. I once spent a very painful weekend learning self-defence. We weren't taught to fight fair!'

Karen laughed, but she was returning to the attack when they were interrupted by the telephone. The sound of Quinn's voice made Camilla flinch, but her own was cool and reserved as she replied to his greeting.

'The weather is supposed to deteriorate again after tomorrow,' he said, 'so how would you and Karen like to come up to the falls with me tomorrow morning? We'll go by Land Rover as it's too wet to take the horses.'

Karen was wildly enthusiastic, so Camilla accepted for her, finishing smoothly, 'Unfortunately I won't be able to come.'

CHAPTER FIVE

'MIGHT I ask why?'

Camilla hesitated, then said in her most wooden tones, 'I have to move some stones around before it rains again.'

Quinn's voice sharpened. 'What stones, Camilla?'

Again she hesitated, avoiding Karen's eyes as she explained what had happened.

There was a taut silence before he said shortly, 'I'll be across at eight tomorrow morning to see what needs to be done.'

'Quinn, I don't need your——'

'I know you'd rather exhaust yourself than accept any help from me,' he interrupted with harsh distinctness, 'but you're going to, anyway. I'll see you at eight.'

She said, 'Thank you,' in her most colourless voice and hung up, turning to face Karen who was viewing her with a quizzical smile. Tonelessly she explained.

Karen laughed outright, primming her mouth.

Through clenched teeth, Camilla said, 'He's an arrogant, bossy, dictatorial swine.'

'I like him, too.'

Camilla stared at her, then relaxed into an unwilling smile. 'You're just as infuriating as he is,' she said.

'You like me, too,' Karen teased.

When she got back to the culvert after milking the next morning, Quinn was already there. He had brought one of the Falls tractors, one with a blade, but the stream bed was too dangerous. With smooth strength he was using a crowbar to manoeuvre the rocks from there to the side of the culvert. When Ben rushed down and greeted him, he stopped to send a daunting glance up at Camilla, who was arrow-straight and guarded on the edge of the culvert.

'Good morning,' he said without expression.

She could be just as cool. 'Good morning,' she returned in her most colourless voice.

Without sparing her another glance, he went back to work, aweing her with the strength in his shoulders and arms as he levered one of the stones free and stretched to lift it into place. She dragged her eyes away from the play of smoothly flexing muscles beneath his shirt, discovering that, although she had the urge to swallow hard, her mouth and throat were suddenly dry. It took all of her courage to jump down from the edge and into the stream bed.

'Stay where you are,' he commanded. As she stopped he observed harshly, 'I suppose you realise that this repair is just as makeshift as the one that was done before? Another really good rain will wash it out again. You need a properly formed culvert with concrete edges.'

'I know. I'll get there one day.'

'One day,' he said grimly, 'might be too late. It's not safe.'

'The tanker driver doesn't seem to mind.'

His broad shoulders lifted in a slight shrug. 'I can't help it if the driver's crazy, that's not my concern. It is not safe for you.'

Somewhere deep inside her a little glow warmed her whole body. She couldn't allow it to mature, so she said stiffly, 'I am not your concern, either.'

Sweat was a light sheen over his forehead; she felt a strange urge to stroke back the darkened lock of chestnut hair that clung to it, but her sense of self-preservation kept her well away from him. And silent.

He rammed a stone into place, and shot her a searing glance. 'Why,' he demanded savagely, 'haven't you had it done properly?'

She should have told him to mind his own business, but he was almost terrifying like this, and so she said in a tone that she was horrified to realise was placating, 'I just can't afford it at the moment, Quinn.'

Another stone went into place and was ferociously rammed in. Then another. This one was bigger, and Camilla watched anxiously as the muscles bulged beneath the thin brushed cotton of his shirt. She had known that he was strong, but she hadn't realised that he possessed this kind of power and brute, raw force. Yet in spite of the disciplined ferocity with which the stones were set in place, he moved gracefully, with a feral flexibility that kept her well away from him.

He didn't have to say anything to her to know that he was in the grip of emotions that needed physical relief. He was more than angry, he was furious. Had he, her guilty mind was quick to suggest, already heard that she had used his name to intimidate the truck-driver the day before?

When the last stone was firmly in place he stood for a moment looking down at his handiwork. Stealing a peep, Camilla thought that she had never seen anyone so icily, implacably in control, and her heart froze in her chest.

Then he looked up, his eyes as green and clear as the edge of a glacier, and pinned her speechless. 'Camilla, will you promise me that if anything else goes wrong you'll let me know?'

In an anguish of indecision, she bit her lip. As her mouth formed a denial, he said harshly, 'I sometimes lie awake wondering whether I'm going to be the one who finds you crushed beneath a tractor because you refuse to admit that there are some things you cannot do without help.'

All colour fled her skin. Her breath jagged through her lungs as she said in a muted voice, 'I have a canopy on this tractor. It's quite safe.'

'That,' he said in a biting voice, 'is not the point.'

Impulsively she started across to him, her hand coming to rest on the taut muscle of his forearm. 'I know, but I'm not stupid,' she said, gripping him urgently to make him understand. 'Honestly, Quinn, if there's anything I don't think I can deal with I'll let you know. I promise.'

His eyes filled her vision, she thought dazedly. They were the green of spring, cool and deep and flecked with gold, and they bored right through her pathetic defences and into her brain, into her heart. The skin beneath her fingertips was heated and smooth above the hard bulge of muscle, and she could smell his scent: musky, salty, ineffably male. Her dry throat threatened to close up entirely, and her heart was thundering so loudly in her chest that she thought she might be suffering some sort of seizure.

Her hand falling to her side, she stepped backwards. The small sounds of the countryside began to impinge once more as her racing heart slowed and quietened. She heard Ben's snuffling sigh, and a chorus of blackbirds in the hedge. A car came up the road and turned into Falls, and one of the cows gave an enquiring bellow.

Quinn was watching her with the mask firmly back in place, his eyes narrowed, his mouth held in a grim straight line. After a moment he said abruptly, 'I'll have to accept that, but if I ever find that you've done anything stupid I swear you'll be eating off the mantelpiece for a week.'

He meant it, too. She swallowed the scratch of fear and said with some of her normal spirit, 'Don't you threaten me.'

'It seems,' he retorted with searing anger, 'to be the only thing you'll listen to.'

The big tractor came in useful for pushing the metal over the reformed road-bed, doing the job in less time than she could have believed possible. She watched until it was finished and he had set off towards Falls, leaving Camilla to walk back to the house.

'I wish I'd seen him,' Karen said enviously. 'I'll bet he strips well.'

She burst out laughing at the dark look her flippancy earned and went to put the toast on, leaving Camilla to shower and try to banish the memory of the way Quinn's body had moved as he'd hoisted the heavy stones into place.

They were ready at ten, Camilla in a pair of dark blue corduroy trousers and a sweatshirt and shirt of the same colour, Karen stunning in warm cream cotton trousers and a caramel-coloured silk shirt, with a deeper caramel jersey over it. Where Camilla wore aged running shoes, Karen's feet and legs were graced by tan boots cut in a vaguely cowboy style. She looked, Camilla thought enviously, very chic in the most casual of ways. Possibly not entirely suitable for a trip in a station Land Rover, but who was going to bother about that?

She did mention that the vehicle was likely to be dirty, but Karen said airily, 'I don't care, I can always get these dry-cleaned. I want to look my best!'

Which Camilla understood. Her heart gave another funny pang when the Land Rover arrived. Accepting that she was attracted to Quinn had been a mistake; it made the attraction grow, like blowing on to kindling. While it had been unrecognised it had smouldered away almost unnoticed but, as soon as she'd let the air at it, it had blazed into a conflagration. It was the most appalling feeling.

As they went the half-mile to Falls her ever-present guilt smeared over the beautiful day. She should not be there, and she should most definitely not be breathing fast because the man behind the wheel was smiling at her. It was useless to try to convince herself that she had no need to feel as though she was betraying both her uncle and her husband; her mind might agree, but her emotions didn't.

Clad in smartly tailored trousers and a cashmere jersey, Mrs Fraser stood waiting in the big machinery yard, apparently conversing with a truck. Camilla leapt out and greeted her with a somewhat harried smile.

'How nice you look,' the older woman said warmly. 'I'm just talking to Dean.'

Camilla bent down. 'The tractor is going perfectly,' she informed the ground.

Dean shot out from under the vehicle, flat on his back on a trolley, and gave her a grin. 'Grand old beasts, those Fergies. Good for another thirty years now.'

Camilla's fervent, 'Oh, I hope so!' made them all but Quinn laugh.

Dean disappeared again, and between the clinks of spanner against machinery came the muffled reply, 'If it doesn't, let me know.'

In Quinn's expression Camilla surprised a look of something that came very close to anger, but as he turned away immediately it might have been her imagination. His voice was certainly perfectly normal when he told them it was time to go.

'I'll sit in the back,' Camilla said, quickly adding as Quinn's glance flicked her way, 'I want to pick your brains, Mrs Fraser. I'd like to make my own cottage cheese and yoghurt, and I know you're an expert.'

It was probably her imagination, but the green eyes seemed to darken. Karen, however, sent her a grateful glance before swinging with alacrity into the front, smiling at Quinn in such open, infectious pleasure that he relaxed and responded in kind.

Falls station was networked by a system of roads, mostly formed and well maintained, with narrower tracks leading off. After a mile or so of easy rolling country the land began to rise towards the hills, outliers of one of the ranges that made Northland's long finger a nightmare to road-builders.

The details of yoghurt culture committed to memory, Camilla looked appreciatively around. 'The country's in good heart,' she said, half to herself.

Mrs Fraser smiled. 'There speaks the landowner. I don't think I've ever seen it look better for the time of year. I suppose we'll pay for it with a drought next summer, but that's the way of the world, isn't it? How are things with you?'

It was a friendly enquiry, but Camilla evaded it with a light laugh. 'Oh, they could be worse. I've just gone on to once-a-day milking, but this time last year I'd dried them off completely. So I'm that much ahead.'

'Good.' Not a hint of pity in her tones, just pleasure because she thought things were working out for her neighbour.

This time last year Dave had just died and Camilla had still been in shock. And now, she thought disconsolately, she felt nothing more than a vast emptiness, as though her life up until now had been worth nothing. She stared at a wood lot, and asked in a quiet voice, 'How old are those pines?'

Without turning his head, Quinn answered, 'Fifteen years. They'll be felled in another five or six.'

So he was listening, in spite of Karen's sparkling conversation. Camilla felt scratchy, angry with herself for being so stupid as to come along on this joy-ride because she had wanted to be close to him.

A short distance on the vehicle drew up beneath an enormous puriri tree that grew against a vertical bluff of purplish-black rock. As soon as the engine died the noise of the falls could be heard—not the ponderous thunder of immense volumes of water, but a silvery splashing, tinkling into the warm sweet air.

'But where are they?' Karen asked, staring around.

'Over the fence and down that way.' Quinn indicated a faint track across the grass that led to a stile.

The path wound down a short slope through the dense shade of more puriri trees until a pool opened out in front of them, almost fifty yards across and longer by half again. At one end a stream ran chuckling over a stony bed towards the lowlands; at the other, a wide sheet of the thinnest gauze spread out across the dark stone, softening and yet emphasising the colour of the rock behind it.

'Oh, that's beautiful,' Karen said softly. 'How deep is the pool?'

'About twenty feet at the deepest.' Quinn's gaze lingered on her lovely face. 'The water is cold, but very refreshing.'

'It looks it!' Karen shuddered delicately. 'What a superb view.'

'In the spring,' Mrs Fraser told them, 'clematis hangs over the cliff in white festoons, and—can you see that patch of darker green over to the left?—that's northern rata. In January it's a great swathe of crimson, and the tuis go mad for it.'

From the grassy bank where they stood, a thin thread of a track wound its way between rocks and low bushes towards the pool. Camilla began to pick her way down, moving slowly, her hands stuffed in the pockets of her utilitarian wind-cheater. Behind her she heard Karen's voice and Quinn's deeper tones in reply. Before she had gone very far, the sounds became blended with the soft chuckling of the water. It was almost as though she was alone, although if she turned her head she would be able to see the slender figure of her cousin and, beside her, tall and protective, that of Quinn. She did not turn her head.

The sun shone across the water, warming dragon-flies in their darting, hovering flight. Camilla perched on a rock conveniently placed to watch one particular insect, a handsome creature with a six-inch wing span and a natty dress of yellow and black stripes.

Slowly, her eyes focusing on the dragon-fly, now on the shimmering expanse of water, occasionally caught by a series of mysterious bubbles that broke the surface and spread in smooth circles, her tension slipped away.

Even under the influence of this most peaceful of scenes, however, she could not banish a last residue of—anger? Pain? Or was it the guilt that spoiled everything? Why had her uncle hated Quinn so fiercely? And why had Dave carried on the feud? She should ask Quinn, but her heart quailed. You're a coward, she told herself with resigned acceptance.

As well ask him if he was deliberately being charming to her in the hope of buying the farm! Of course, it would be simple to find out if that was true. All she had to do was tell him that if she sold to him she lost all her rights to the farm, and would be left to pay off the debt that Dave had incurred with the bank. Then stand back and wait for results, she thought cynically, refusing to ask herself what stopped her from doing exactly that.

About fifty yards past the pool the hint of a track turned up the bank to lead on to a small, grassy plateau. Driven by her thoughts, Camilla got up and strode along it, to stop on the edge and look about her in silence. A little distance away belladonnas bloomed, their naked stems thrust up through the grass to hold pink and white trumpets aloft. Beyond them in patches of darker green were arum lilies, velvet white cornucopias with a spathe of bold yellow. Camilla made a small sound of pleasure.

Behind her, Quinn said, 'Fifty years ago this used to be a shepherd's cottage.'

All that was left was an old brick chimney pointing a gaunt finger to the sky, and two gnarled apple trees with small red fruit clinging to the lichened branches. To one side a lemon tree still had a few golden fruit hanging from thin, frail twigs.

Without turning, she asked, 'Are there daffodils here in the spring?'

'Yes, old-fashioned ones, with jonquils and great clumps of snowflakes. And little purple-backed freesias have naturalised around the trunks of the apple trees.'

A fine thread of tension spun out between them. It was so still, so quiet, that she and Quinn could have been the only people in the world. One of the dogs came panting up the hill and sat down in the nearest patch of shade.

The hair on the back of her neck lifted; to break the spell she walked across to the apple tree and picked one of the small fruit, polishing it on the leg of her jeans.

She bit into it, relishing its sweet crispness, and turned. Quinn had followed her across and was standing a few feet away. He picked a fruit too, and gave it to her, smiling. While she burnished it he took the one she had already bitten and ate it, his strong white teeth making short work of the faintly golden flesh.

Something very strange happened to her heart while an equally potent sorcery worked a magic on her body. She leaned back against the trunk, unable to drag her eyes away from his face, listening to the bees humming in the throats of the belladonnnas at her feet. Above the cool murmuration of the falls a skylark sang, ecstasy translated to music.

His eyes were lit from within by a flame that was paradoxically hot and cold at the same time. With her breath imprisoned in her throat, Camilla tried to calm her racing pulses by considering the subtle nuances of heredity. Her own hair was black, yet the sunlight summoned blue fire from it, whereas Quinn's gleamed with the fires of passion. Or of hell, she thought dazedly, eating the apple he had given her. It was the devil who had seduced Eve with an apple.

Perhaps their differing colouring was an indication of their temperaments. Blue was a cool colour, reserved, subdued, but the chestnut and flame of autumn denoted warmth and passion.

He said softly, 'You have eyes like crystals. Cold and clear and sparkling.'

In a husky voice she replied, 'I hate them. They're so colourless, it's as though there's no one behind them.'

'Is that how you feel?'

She bit her lip. 'No, of course not.'

But it was. She had never been just Camilla. Her mother used to say that she was her reason for living, then she had become her nurse, her stay against the miseries of illness and death. Then she had been Dave's wife; now she was his widow.

The green eyes were narrow and hard. 'I find you utterly maddening, do you know that? I can never tell what you are thinking, or what you will do.'

She asked, 'Why did Dave dislike you so?'

The abrupt question didn't throw him. Eyes narrowed to pin-points of brilliance, he replied, 'You know perfectly well that Dave didn't dislike me. He hated me.'

Reluctantly, she inclined her head. 'But why? It can't have been because Uncle Philip disliked you.'

'No. It had nothing to do with your uncle.'

'And you're not going to tell me,' she supplied on a tired inflection.

For a moment she thought he might. He paused, his eyes unsparing and enigmatic as they searched her face. But, 'No, you're not ready to hear it. Beyond the fact that we had reason enough for our mutual dislike.'

She gasped. 'You didn't hate Dave.'

A cruel little smile curled his mouth. For a moment he looked as forbidding and ruthless as the Trojan warrior who had killed her namesake, the warrior queen, thousands of years before. 'Not enough to wish him dead,' he said, incredibly. His eyes bored into hers. 'Believe that, if you don't believe anything else.'

Horrified, she stammered, 'Of course I believe you!'

He gave a short laugh and seemed to be about to say something more, but was interrupted by the sound of voices coming closer. With relief that she couldn't hide, Camilla turned to smile at them.

Karen looked from one to the other, her eyes very sharp, but all that she said was a laughing, 'You're looking very Lady-of-Shalott-ish, Cam.'

'"A curse has come upon me"?' Camilla threw her apple core neatly into a bush, where one of the dogs found it and swallowed it in a great gulp, before spitting

PEEK-A-BOO!

Free Gifts For You!

Look inside—Right Now! We've got something special just for you!

GIFTS

*There's no cost—
and no obligation
to buy anything!*

We'd like to send you free gifts to thank you for being a romance reader, and to introduce you to the benefits of the Harlequin Reader Service®: free home delivery of brand-new Harlequin Presents® novels months before they're available in stores, and at a savings from the cover price!

Accepting our free gifts places you under no obligation to buy anything ever. You may cancel the Reader Service at any time, even just after receiving your free gifts, simply by writing "cancel" on your statement or returning a shipment of books to us at our cost. But if you choose not to cancel, every month we'll send you six more Harlequin Presents® novels, and bill you just $2.24* apiece—and there's **no** extra charge for shipping and handling. There are **no** hidden extras!

the pips out with comical precision. 'Hardly. I've been admiring the scenery.'

Mrs Fraser looked up at the towering cliff above them. 'Do you remember the first time you climbed the bluff, Quinn?'

'I do indeed. I was about ten or eleven, I think.'

'You were a very headstrong nine,' his mother informed him severely. 'Iron-willed, independent, and with no regard for maternal fears.'

He grinned. 'You didn't know about it until afterwards.'

'The story of my life as a mother,' she returned crisply. 'Just as well, I suppose, or I'd have died a thousand deaths before you reached the age of discretion.'

Karen cast him a laughing sideways glance. 'Have you reached the age of discretion? Poor Quinn.'

He enjoyed the innuendo, although he didn't reply beyond a quirk of his brows and a smile that made Karen's lashes flicker. Camilla had to turn away, because even that made her raw with jealousy. He didn't seem to reciprocate Karen's interest; he certainly enjoyed her flirtatious manner, but not even Camilla with her newfound propensity for obsession could discern anything more in his attitude to her cousin than pleasure in her company and enjoyment of her stunning good looks.

On the way back Karen pleaded prettily with Quinn for a moonlight picnic at the falls. 'Not now, it's too cold, but perhaps in the summer...?'

'Will you be here in the summer?' he asked lazily.

She smiled. 'I hope so. I'm sick of living in Auckland. If I can find a job in Bowden, Cam says I can live with her.'

'An excellent idea,' he approved.

From behind Camilla saw the groove in his cheek as he smiled, and wondered dismally whether her reading of the situation was wrong. Perhaps if Karen was living in the district he might further the acquaintance. Would the moonlight picnic be an affair for two people only?

Back at the homestead she yielded to her hostess's suggestion that they eat lunch there. She even produced a smile when she did it, and hoped that it hid successfully the wild turmoil that stopped her brain from producing one sensible thought.

Once inside the house, however, Quinn requested that she go with him to the office, as they had business to discuss. A swift glance revealed that his expression had hardened into purposefulness.

The room was dominated by a large desk. Knowing from her own experience just how much paperwork would be needed to run a station this size, Camilla cast it a respectful glance, more than a little intimidated by its neatness. Her own desk tended to lurk beneath an avalanche of forms and papers. But then Quinn employed a secretary.

And he wore his clothes with the kind of fastidiousness that denoted an aversion to clutter. Even now, casually clad in khaki trousers and a dark green shirt, he looked like an idealised gentleman farmer. Only the controlled strength, the bred-in-the-bone confidence informed those who met him that he was one of those rare creatures whose striking physical presence was backed up by a tough, implacable authority. A born leader, she supposed, watching him from beneath her lashes.

Suddenly stifling, she walked across the room to stand at the french window. Her gaze travelled across a flagstoned terrace to an enormous tree that flamed like a pyramid of scarlet in the lawn. Among the leaves she could see the golden globes of its fruit, the persimmon, savagely astringent unless it was truly ripe.

'Well?' she asked aggressively. 'What do you want?'

His hand on her shoulder made her jump. He turned her to face him, not forcefully, but the touch of his fingers reawakened the bruises of the day before, and she had to catch back an exclamation of pain.

'What have you done to yourself?' he demanded, his fingers massaging the sore flesh.

Pushing hands that trembled into her pocket, she moved away, hunching an ungracious shoulder at him.

'Nothing. What—don't, Quinn!' She whipped her hands up to pull his away from the buttons of her blouse, but it was too late, the top two were unfastened and he was spreading the soft material back to reveal the bruises that marred the translucent pallor of her skin. She knew what he was seeing; in her mirror that morning the fingerprints had stood out like black marks of shame.

For a moment they stood very still, Camilla watching his face with terrified fascination as it darkened into fury. When he spoke it was between his teeth, in a voice so silky soft that she barely heard it. 'Who did this to you?'

'I—it's none of your business.'

His eyes flicked up and she almost cried out at the cold and controlled menace she saw there. 'A lover, Camilla? Do you enjoy violence?'

Her lips were stiff with fear. 'No,' she whispered. 'I have no lover.'

'Then who?'

'Quinn, it's not anything to do with you. I'm not hurt. I—I set Ben on him and threatened him with——' But she stopped, for she could hardly tell him that she had used his name to threaten the driver. He was a protective man, his strength tempered by gentleness, but she had always recognised a primitive streak in him, recognised it and feared it, and she was facing it now.

'Who was it?'

His hands moved, spreading the collar further, touching the bruises with gentle fingers that belied his black fury. Even in her fear Camilla reacted with the hot sizzle of excitement that his touch always brought. Lifting her hands, she dragged ineffectually at his.

'Tell me!' he repeated with harsh insistence. 'I can easily find out.'

Of course he could. Karen would tell him if he asked. But in spite of the fact that the driver deserved to be punished, she didn't want Quinn to be the agent.

She admitted cautiously, 'It was the driver of the quarry truck. He just got a little—overexcited.'

He was looking down at the marks, his fingers moving in wonderful gentleness over the discoloured skin. After a few seconds the tension that held her stiffly erect began to seep away. She had to fight an overpowering urge to rest her head on that broad shoulder and relax against him, accept without demur the protection he was offering. His touch was soft and sensuously soothing, stroking across the skin as though he loved the feel of it.

Cold common sense flooded through her. Careless of her dignity, she managed to jerk away, and with shaking fingers pulled the collar of her shirt up and refastened the buttons. Her voice made a brave stab at wry amusement. 'It happens, Quinn. A certain sort of man thinks that all young widows are on the lookout for sex. They don't persist when I make it clear they're wrong.'

She had never seen a man look so forbidding. The angles and planes of his face could have been sculptured from granite, cold and relentless and completely daunting. And his eyes! They should have been icy cold, but she could see a flame smouldering in the green depths like the fire at the heart of an emerald, a blaze of emotion barely contained by his will.

His voice was still the silken texture of extreme rage. 'But you had to set the dog on this one to make yourself clear?'

'Some,' she ventured with a small, peaceable smile, 'take a little convincing.'

'Who was he?'

'I don't know.'

'His name will be on the job sheet.' He was icily inexorable.

She said uncertainly, 'Quinn, it was an isolated incident. He won't try it again.'

'How the hell do you know that?' he demanded through set lips. 'If he used enough force to produce bruises like that, rape could well mean nothing to him. You haven't the slightest idea of the effect you have on a man. You're about as worldly as a ten-year-old child.'

'Worldly enough to know that he didn't have rape on his mind,' she retorted acidly. A quick yank at her shirt tucked it further into her jeans, a measure of courage mixed with defiance pulled her shoulders straight.

Apparently unmoved, he was reaching for the telephone directory.

'Don't interfere,' she said, clearly and angrily. 'You have no right to mix yourself up in my affairs.'

Hardly the best word to use, but it didn't matter because he ignored her. In a curt, level voice he gave the number of the quarry office. She began to object further, but he silenced her with an arctic state, inflexible and decisive, that chilled her to the bone.

'Quinn Fraser here. Could I speak to Don, please?'

Of course he could speak to Don, she thought hysterically. Quinn Fraser would probably be put straight through to the Prime Minister.

'Don? I have something to discuss with you in private. When would be a good time?' He paused, and the frown deepened. 'Yes. Yes. Very well, I'll see you then.' He hung up and turned to face her again, his eyes narrowed and watchful.

Crisp and businesslike, Camilla thought savagely, and very much the man in control. And she hoped desperately that he would never learn that she had used his name to threaten the driver.

He said bluntly, 'Didn't it occur to you that one night when he's drunk and feeling reckless he might come looking for you?'

It hadn't, or at least not that she had recognised. At this open enunciation of fears hidden even from herself she felt a coldness on her skin and knew that she had gone pale. She turned away, but it was too late. He had noticed, and he would push home the advantage.

Making a brave effort to retrieve her position, she said curtly, 'I'm not that stupid. I lock the doors, and Ben would give tongue if anyone set foot on the place.'

'So you would know he was coming,' he returned with uncompromising scorn. 'But you keep the dog tied up outside at night. Anyone could ignore his barking and climb in through a window left unlocked.'

'If I was stupid enough to let him, then yes, I suppose anyone could.'

His eyes came to rest on the place where her shirt hid her bruises. 'You haven't exactly reassured me that you're capable of resisting,' he pointed out acidly. 'And, while I've no doubt you would put up a good fight, a really determined man would overcome you in a fairly short time, even with the dog barking his head off outside.'

'Karen——'

'Is not going to be home always.' He smiled without humour. 'Correct me if I'm wrong, but she strikes me as being a social soul, one of those people who enjoy going out and meeting people.'

'So what do you expect me to do?' Drawing an uneven breath, she moved across to the window, staring unseeingly out.

'Well, the first thing to do is make it obvious that anyone who thinks of visiting will have me to deal with.'

She laughed without amusement. 'In other words, that I'm under your protection? I've already...' Her voice trailed away as she realised, too late, what she had said.

'You've already what?'

Touching her tongue to her dry lips, she cursed her unruly tongue. 'I—threatened him with losing his job.'

'And?'

'He said that it was his word against mine.'

'And?' he repeated inexorably.

The words were gall in her mouth. 'I sort of mentioned your name.' Her cheeks burned at the memory of the driver's response.

From behind her Quinn said evenly, 'So you gave me the right to interfere.'

She swung around, her face truculent. 'OK, so I used your name to threaten him. I'm sorry. I know I shouldn't have done it—I didn't want to get you mixed up——'

'It was the most sensible thing you could do,' he said calmly, taking the wind entirely out of her sails.

Her eyes flew to his, met understanding and even sympathy in the crystalline depths. She gulped and said in a voice that was too unsteady, 'It wasn't. It was an awful cheek, and cowardly of me, and I feel like a worm for doing it, but don't you see? If you get him sacked it will only confirm what he thought, and I'm sorry,' she said, the words tangling in her mouth.

'And what did he think?'

Her colour deepened and she couldn't meet his eyes.

'I see.' He didn't sound angry. He didn't sound anything. When she peeped up through her lashes she was surprised to see that his expression was controlled and remote, as though he was thinking furiously.

In a small voice she said again, 'I'm sorry.'

'I prefer you spitting fire and fury to stumbling over profuse and unnecessary apologies,' he remarked with a bite that he didn't try to hide.

She slanted him a worried look, wondering why he wasn't totally, savagely furious with her for embroiling him in something as distasteful as this. 'But you do see, don't you, that if you get him sacked it will only confirm any conclusions he's come to?'

'Leave it to me.'

She said angrily, 'No, I can't do that.'

'How,' he enquired with deadly smoothness, 'are you going to stop me?'

While she stared at him in baffled anger, he smiled down at her with a cynically amused recognition of her predicament that won an answering gleam from her. Ruthlessly subduing it, she ignored the strange sensations that prickled along her nerves. 'You want too much,' she blurted.

A spark of danger flared in his eyes, then died—or was controlled—as swiftly as it had come. 'Do you think so?' he asked without inflection. 'I've never asked anything of you, Camilla, except a little trust.'

'And the farm.'

CHAPTER SIX

THE silence seemed eternal as she saw the charm transmuted into ruthlessness. It was a change that Camilla welcomed. It would not do to forget that he could be as tough as any paladin of the Dark Ages intent on forging himself a realm out of chaos by brute force and cunning.

'But you don't want to sell,' Quinn observed, but without emphasis, almost as though her answer held little interest for him.

A tide of weakness almost overcame her. For the space of a few heartbeats she was sorely tempted to give in. The incident with the driver had shaken her confidence and she was tired, so tired that even the thought of having to pay off the debts on the property seemed the lesser of the evils that confronted her.

Then sanity reasserted itself. And guilt. How could she let the property fall into Quinn's hands? Closing her eyes for a moment, she saw Dave's agonised face as he made her promise not to sell to Quinn. The words had been groaned out, slurred through a miasma of pain and analgesics, the strength summoned from some deep inner resource because he'd known that he was dying.

'Not—Quinn...' he had gasped. 'Promise me...'

She would have promised him anything, but even though her vow was unfairly extracted under the awful duress of death, she could not go back on her word now. It would be the grossest disloyalty.

'No.'

Quinn wasn't surprised. Not a muscle in his face moved, yet his anger was a palpable force in the quiet room. Her chin lifted. She gave him back a look that dared him to continue.

He said without emphasis, 'It's too much for you. If you sold you could buy a smaller place, closer to town.'

In a harsh voice she repeated, 'No.'

He measured the strength of her determination with a long, high-nosed stare that gave no quarter. As if coming to some conclusion, he said coolly, 'No one else will buy the place from you.'

She blinked. 'Why?'

'Because I've already let all the land agents know that if the property changes hands I'll close the road beyond my gate. I can do it, Camilla. It's a private road from my boundary. If you sell to anyone other than me, I'll make sure they have no way of getting on to the farm.'

Fired by his ruthlessness, she flashed, 'What stops you from closing the road off now?'

'This,' he said, the word deep and thick in his throat as he came towards her.

She stepped back, but it was too late, and she was locked in his arms while his mouth took hers with no gentleness, no subtlety. He wanted to do one thing, impress upon her how helpless she was in his arms, and he did that very well, forcing her head back with the power of his kiss until her throat was stretched and painful.

Unbidden, unwanted, from somewhere deep inside her a wildfire response fountained up through her body. She only just managed to restrain it, but nothing could stop the deep inner trembling that had her mindlessly in thrall.

After a moment the fierce pressure slackened and he gathered her quiescent body closer. She would have had to be very innocent indeed not to recognise the power and urgency of his desire. She flinched away, but he made a deep soothing sound in his throat and suddenly she was no longer outraged, although her fear deepened.

Camilla did not respond, but neither did she struggle. A kind of lassitude held her still as his mouth plundered hers; a strange inevitability kept her prisoner. Repressed needs stirred, sharpened by the time that had passed since last she had indulged them, apparent in the rapid pulsing of her body and the sweet temptation to surrender. Her lips softened, began to make their own demands. Quinn responded with a sudden ferocity that stopped her heart.

Dimly, through the flood of passion so urgently and unexpectedly brought to life, she understood that this was what had kept her so wary. In some hidden region of her being she had known right from the start that she could respond to him like this, and the knowledge had frightened her because she had felt nothing like it with Dave.

'Open your mouth,' he said thickly. 'Open your mouth for me.'

A strange heat ran from her breasts to the hidden juncture of her thighs. She could no more have denied him than run away, because denying him meant denying herself, and more than food and drink, more than self-respect, more than life itself, she wanted him and what he was doing to her untried body. Her lips parted, and she shuddered at the instant probe, the searching exploration that made her bones feel as though they were stuffed with wool. He tasted of male, wild and unconstrained, the cool control she had thought to be so characteristic of him lost in a haze of primal, masculine passion.

And then she was free, standing dazed while Mrs Fraser's voice drifted in through the french windows, almost drowning out the frustrated imprecation that came from the man releasing her.

Straightening the collar of her shirt with fingers that shook, he said tonelessly, 'I'm not going to apologise.

You wanted it just as much as I did, so don't go whipping
up a false anger because you think you owe it to your
pride.'

Sheer self-preservation forced the words from her
mouth. 'My anger is far from spurious, I can assure you.
I don't resent the kiss so much as the attitude that led
to it. Droit de seigneur, if it ever existed, went out in
the Middle Ages.'

Her voice was as dispassionate as she could make it,
but there was an ominous wobble in the last word that
silenced her. Aching with frustrated passion, she took a
deep breath and watched angrily as he slid a sheaf of
papers together and put them into a folder.

'May we come in?' Mrs Fraser followed hard on the
heels of her enquiry. After one swift glance at Quinn,
now the full width of the desk away from Camilla, she
went on cheerfully, 'I've just been showing Karen around
the garden. Have you finished, or shall we go away
again?'

As he straightened up Quinn's glance lingered a
moment on Camilla's averted profile before he answered,
'No, we've finished for the time being.'

Karen's voice was light and her expression half-teasing
as she said, 'Oh, this is a continuing discussion, is it?'

'When you share a common boundary there is always
business to be discussed.' He smiled at her, ruthlessly
using his charm, then asked, 'Is there any lunch?'

'We have,' his mother told him very drily, 'been
waiting for you.'

They ate on one of the side terraces, a small, intimate
space paved with old bricks, the edges softened with
alyssum. The furniture was comfortable, white-painted
cane padded with large cushions in shades of blue and
green and lilac. Camilla managed to eat, but she didn't
taste anything. She was too blazingly aware of the man

who sat beside her, very sure of himself, relaxed, amusing, exciting; perhaps only she noticed that he was also watchful, making sure that Karen was too busy responding to his blatant charm to notice Camilla's silence.

She tried to tell herself that he was ignoring her, but her instincts didn't play her false. The weight of his attention was like a heated golden cloak around her; his efforts to keep the conversational ball away from her sprang from a strong protectiveness that insensibly warmed her. Yet as the minutes ticked by she found herself becoming more and more wary, the memory of those minutes spent in his arms taking on an ominous importance.

When at last he dropped them off at the house she was almost indecently relieved, a relief that turned to annoyance when he rested a negligent hand on her shoulder and, with mockery lighting his eyes, told her that he'd be in touch soon.

She had no idea what reply she made, but when they got inside Karen commented, 'I thought you didn't know him very well.'

'I don't.'

'Well, the air certainly sizzles when you're together. What on earth were you quarrelling about?'

'He made an offer for the farm.'

Karen surveyed her closely, her expression hard to read. 'I see,' she said. After a few moments she resumed, 'Why don't you tell him that you can't afford to sell to him?'

The corners of Camilla's mouth tucked in. 'What would be the use?'

'He would at least understand why you're so adamant.'

Camilla began to feel hunted. She shrugged. 'It wouldn't make any difference. I'd have to tell him that

I owe so much on the place I can't repay the debt. It seems—disloyal to Dave.'

Karen said thoughtfully, 'You know, I think you're using it to keep some sort of barrier between you.'

Her astuteness made Camilla flinch. Quickly, before she had time to think, she demanded, 'Why would I want to do that?'

'Because you want him?'

Camilla looked at her as though she was crazy. 'Don't be an idiot.'

'You'd be the idiot if you hadn't noticed that he is an extraordinarily attractive man,' Karen reurned crisply. 'Come on, Cam, he has to be the biggest hunk I've seen for years, if ever. And the fact that his looks are the least of his assets make him infinitely more desirable. Real fantasy stuff—charm, and money, and authority. You're a woman—if nothing else, your hormones must have informed you that he's a man, and one who is damned good in bed.'

Camilla's hands flew to her hot cheeks. 'OK,' she said in a stifled voice, 'so he's attractive. He's also not in the least interested in me.'

'If you're so sure of that, why don't you tell him you can't sell to him? That way you'll know, one way or another. Unless,' her cousin finished slyly, 'you don't want to risk driving him away!'

'I do!' Camilla almost shouted at her, hiding with a show of anger her reaction to the accuracy of this shot. 'I mean, I don't! Oh, hell, of course he wants the farm. As well as all those other attributes you dwell on so lovingly, don't forget that Quinn's a damned good businessman. He's probably not above using a little light flirtation to get what he wants!'

The other woman looked at her thoughtfully. 'So he did make a pass at you. I'm beginning to think you're blind, Cam. Are you telling me that he's the sort of swine who would deliberately use his flagrant charm to seduce a poor widow out of her inheritance?'

Camilla bit her lip. 'No,' she said carefully. 'He wouldn't cheat me, because he's offered me more than the land is worth. He thinks I'm crazy to want to live here, and he's sure that he knows better than I do what is good for me. So he doesn't think of it as seducing me into anything; he's just sweetening me up for my own good.'

'I see.' Karen smiled obliquely, then said with a rather astonished laugh, 'Well, my mixed-up cousin, I think I'm withdrawing from the contest.'

'What do you mean?'

Shaking her head, Karen headed off for her bedroom. 'How you've managed to reach the ripe old age of twenty-two and remain so naïve I'll never know. I don't get mixed up in other people's battles.'

'You've got it all wrong!' Camilla glared at the door as it closed gently. Why didn't Karen realise that Quinn saw her as a thorn in his side who had to be sweetened into selling to him?

She stamped into her own bedroom, vowing that she was never going to be alone in Quinn Fraser's company again. Karen was welcome to him! Ruthlessly banishing all memories of her incandescent reaction to his love-making, she changed into working clothes and went off down the paddock, ridding herself of some of the be-wildering complex of emotions swirling around inside her by attacking several gorse bushes that had found their way into the farm.

When she had finished she leaned, puffing heavily, on the handle of the slasher and looked around. Compared to the manicured paddocks of Falls, hers were showing a lack of money and attention. During the preceding years the interest repayments to the bank had eaten up most of the money that would have been spent on fertilisers, and the differing greens of the grass on each side of the boundary showed that the pastures were beginning to degrade. Biting her lip, she sent Ben off to round up the cows.

The next day the last cheque of the season from the Dairy Company was paid into her bank account. She would have to wait for the bonus pay-out, and after that it would be six weeks or so before the first cheque of the new season came in. Panic rose in her, and as she had so often done before she forced it back. Panic caused muddled thinking, and she couldn't afford that. But she would have to see the bank manager immediately—no more cravenly putting it off.

'Coming into town this afternoon?' she asked Karen at lunchtime.

'Yes.' Her cousin hesitated, before saying carefully, 'Do you really want me to come and live here? Be honest, Cam. I don't want you to say yes and then get sick of me. I'll pay my share of the expenses, of course, and do my bit around the house.'

Camilla said eagerly, 'Yes, I'd like it. We get on well, don't we? I could do with the company, and the help, quite frankly. If it doesn't work out, we'll say so and part without quarrelling.' She smiled. 'Two sensible people should be able to share a house without too much trouble.'

Karen's eyes twinkled at some private joke. 'So they should,' she said. 'I'll ask around the shops this afternoon and see what sort of jobs there are.'

Camilla thought she'd have no difficulty. Karen was very attractive, but more to the point she looked chic and elegant, dressing with style and flair. Any shop in Bowden would be pleased to hire her.

As Camilla showered before going in she looked at her hands, smiling wryly at the havoc two days spent picking tomatoes had wreaked. The nails were now short and filed straight across, and even the most vigorous scrubbing hadn't been able to get rid of the faint yellowish stain. She had worn gloves, but somehow the stain managed to seep in and her white skin showed up every little mark.

At least her bruises were gone. But thinking about the bruises invariably led to recalling that confrontation in Quinn's office, and the flare of passion that had temporarily overcome her common sense. She had tried to thrust it to the back of her mind. If she thought too much about it she might start remembering things that were better left forgotten, like the feel of his body, taut and hard and powerful, overpowering hers so that she felt small and fragile and weak. Or the taste of him on her tongue, darkly mysterious; or the wildfire response he summoned from her...

Repressing the memories had been difficult, because he had done something more fundamental than kiss her. He had woken her into life from a long sleep, and things could never be the same again. Like a coward, she refused to explore that idea, too. She was getting rather good at censoring her thoughts. Live for each day, she told herself, that was what she must do. It was as good a name as any for a wilful refusal to face what had happened.

In Bowden they went their separate ways, Camilla first to the supermarket, to buy only the most basic of necessities. On her way back to the car she stopped at the window of one of the dress shops. Shades of plum and violet were the fashion this season. Her eyes slipped longingly across tweed skirts and lambswool jerseys, little waistcoats in dark jewel colours, long boots in leather to match the clothes, and bright tights, all pretty and warm and expensive.

She looked down a moment at her jeans and sweat-shirt. Not even by economising fantastically could she afford anything of the wares so temptingly displayed, as the bank manager would no doubt tell her in ten minutes or so.

Quinn's voice came mockingly across her shoulder. 'What are you going to buy?'

She jumped and swivelled around. 'I—none,' she said, trying not to react so sharply to his potent masculinity.

He said provocatively, 'If you sold to me you could buy the whole windowful. That crimson skirt and jersey would suit you perfectly, although I think I like you best in violet. It gives a certain mysterious sensuality to your eyes.'

Colouring, she said, 'Get thee behind me, Satan.'

His smile was a taunt, but he held out an imperative hand for the groceries. Handing them over, she won-dered how he got away with walking along the street carrying a shopping bag that had definitely seen better days without losing any of the lithe masculine grace that she admired so much. Charisma, she decided glumly.

Back at the car he opened the boot and deposited the bag inside, before saying, 'I spoke to Don Jameson at the quarry. He was, naturally, extremely concerned and is dealing with the situation. Discreetly, of course.'

She reacted predictably to the sarcasm. 'Of course. Thank you so much for your patronage.'

'Is that how it seems to you?'

Ignoring the warning note in his voice, she retorted, 'Yes. How else could it seem?'

'One neighbour helping another?'

'Unwanted, unasked-for help, however kindly meant, is interfering patronage,' she said stiffly, impelled to force him back behind the barriers that had kept them apart before. She was in danger, from herself as well as him, and she would do anything to keep him at a safe distance.

He looked down at her with an impassive expression. Her skin tightened and she had to stop herself from taking a tiny step backwards. He smiled grimly, but something behind her caught his attention and the smile was transformed into a real one.

Sure enough, it was Karen, approaching with a triumphant grin. 'Hello, Quinn. Congratulate me, both of you. The boutique needs a full-time saleswoman. I start at the beginning of next week. The only thing that perturbs me a bit is how I'm going to get in and out.'

His answering smile was warm and openly appreciative. 'Congratulations. Bowden will be infinitely more colourful for your presence here. As for a lift, one of the shepherd's daughters works in town, and I'm sure she'd be happy to have someone share petrol expenses with her. You can't take Camilla's old heap; it's a terminal case.'

The shadow in Camilla's eyes deepened. The well-being of her car was one of the worries that haunted her on sleepless nights. A vehicle was a necessity, and it was a miracle that bits of the old thing hadn't dropped off, vital parts that would cost her a pretty penny to repair. Sooner or later it would happen. But that was another of the fears that she pushed to the back of her mind.

She listened with a set smile as Karen sparkled up at Quinn, responding to his unforced masculinity with open admiration. Camilla smiled and nodded and felt more and more conspicuous by the minute, until at last Quinn said that he had to be going, and gave her a coolly dismissive smile in contrast to the warmth of his farewell to Karen.

He was only two steps away when Karen asked, 'What did the bank manager say?'

'Hush!' Was it her imagination, or had Quinn's stride hesitated a moment?

'Oh, sorry, although what on earth harm can it do if he knows you're going to see the man? I thought every farmer practically lived in the bank manager's office these days. You're becoming paranoid, Cam.'

Patiently, she said, 'I'm on the way now.'

Karen gave her a sustaining and sympathetic look. 'OK. I'll wait for you in the coffee shop.'

Of course Quinn was nowhere in sight when she got to the bank, and she was so busy scolding herself for looking for him that she almost forgot to be nervous when the bank manager invited her into his office. He was middle-aged and fatherly, but she knew that he had not reached this level by being foolishly kind, and although she had made out as good a case for herself as she could she was dismally certain that no man in his position would see her as a good risk. However, she took a deep breath, only to be interrupted by the impatient summons of the telephone.

'I'm sorry, Mrs Evans.' He lifted the receiver and barked his name. The frown died immediately. 'Yes,' he said formally. 'No, it's all right. Yes.'

Camilla sat perched on the edge of her chair, tense and desperate, while he listened intently. He was one of those people who looked in one direction when on the telephone, and he seemed to have chosen Camilla for his point of reference, watching her with narrowed concentration while the person at the other end spoke. If it hadn't been so impersonal a stare, she would have shrivelled.

But at last he said, 'No. You know I can't do—oh, I see. Well, provided it's understood—ah, yes, that's quite different. Yes. Yes, of course. I understand. Goodbye.' He put the receiver down and smiled. 'I'm sorry about that, Mrs Evans, but it was important. Now, what can I do for you?'

He was affable, listening carefully so that she found herself gaining confidence, and as she showed him figures and accounts he seemed almost sympathetic. But she held her breath when she made her request, insensibly stiffening herself for a refusal.

Almost incredulously she heard him say, 'Yes, I think we can do that for you. Although we'll need to keep a close watch on your outgoings.'

She bit her lip. 'Do you mean you want to put me on a budget?'

'Not exactly. You appear to be doing a very good, very sensible job. I'd just like to know if in future you have anything like this, any unexpected expenses, so that we can deal with them in the most suitable manner.'

She felt euphoric. Of course she now had to worry about paying the extra loan off, but surely something would go well for her this year? With Karen paying her share of the expenses the burden would be a little easier to bear, and there was talk of the final pay-out from the Dairy Company this year being higher than expected.

That night they shared a bottle of wine. 'To celebrate,' Karen said as she produced it, 'the bank manager's moment of kindness! And the new job.'

The following day dawned with a pall of cloud hanging low, cloud that turned to a drizzling cold rain by lunchtime. As the weather came in from the east it was slow to move away, so the following days were gloomy. Camilla stayed inside except for the necessary jobs, but there were enough of these to keep her wet and windblown. Her work at the market gardens was hard and exhausting, a grind that slowed her down and made her bones ache each night. Occasionally she found herself wondering wistfully if she would ever be able to give up working there, but a natural, though sorely pressed optimism convinced her that it would happen, some time. She was now beginning to look ahead, instead of plodding mindlessly from one day to the next.

Returning from moving the springing heifers one afternoon, she noticed Quinn's Jaguar parked outside the house. She concentrated on the squelch of her boots in the grass and thought dourly that it was just as well that she didn't hope he was there to see her, otherwise she might be upset with the fact that her hair was wet and her face slick with cold and rain.

Restraining the butterflies that had taken wing in her stomach, she tied Ben up and made her way into the back porch, hanging up oilskins and boots before picking her way past the deep-freeze to the tub in the laundry. After scrubbing her hands, she ran a comb through her hair, ruthlessly dragging the wet mass back off her face, then walked up the two steps to the back door, her face set.

The kitchen table was warm and tidy, the vase of jonquils on the table scenting the air. From behind the half-open door into the sitting-room came Karen's laugh, warmly intimate, followed by her raised voice.

'Is that you, Cam?'

'Yes. I won't be a moment.'

With unnecessary clatter she filled the electric kettle and plugged it in, then began to butter the scones that Karen had made in the morning.

Karen said cheerfully, 'I can do that, Cam. Quinn wants to talk to you, so I'll finish here.'

Camilla gave her an uncertain glance, but Karen's eyes were limpid, even amused. 'Thanks,' she said.

Rubbing her hands down the side seams of her jeans smoothed away the dampness in her palms, but it took all her will-power to fake some sort of confidence. And when she saw him standing by the fireplace, the strong angles and planes of his face highlighted by the warmth and glow of the flames, she realised how much she had dreaded seeing him again. And how much she had longed to.

He was looking at a book that he had taken from one of the shelves which filled the niches on either side of the fireplace, and queried as she came into the room, 'Are you the science fiction addict?'

'Yes.'

'Something we have in common.' The book, closed with a snap, was replaced. She watched the deft movement of his hands and felt a liquid sensation in her stomach. He went on without expression, 'I've been in contact with Don Jameson. After asking around he's discovered several women who have been intimidated by the driver's behaviour. A few days ago he overstepped the mark with a teenager, and was the subject of a complaint. He's been sacked, and told to leave the district or he'll face prosecution for indecent assault. So you won't be seeing him again.'

Until then Camilla had not realised how much she had dreaded a further meeting with the man. Her relief blazed forth from her face as she said huskily, 'I see. I'm glad. Has he gone?'

'Yes.' His eyes were shards of emerald as they scanned her face.

Unease walked on stealthy footsteps through her mind. Preserving her impassive countenance, she said, 'So you needn't have got mixed up in it.'

He smiled inimically. 'No. It's just as well that I didn't expect any gratitude, isn't it?'

His determination to make her feel small fired her temper, causing a tiny muscle to flick in the smooth line of her jaw. She took a firm hold on herself and said calmly, 'I was thinking of you. It wouldn't have done your reputation any good to have your name linked with mine in such an unsavoury situation.'

'I'd have survived.'

The cold sarcasm made her stiffen. After a swift glance at the uncompromising harshness of his features, she said quietly, 'Thank you, anyway.'

'For the interference? Or the patronage?'

Her tentative smile died stillborn. She stared at him with a wounded expression, but his face didn't change, not a muscle moving in the handsome bronze mask. A log of wood hissed, sending out a jet of flame, and the light flared across his face, lending him a polished, sinister menace. The muscles moved in Camilla's throat as she swallowed. She thought of Lucifer, and for the first time in her life she knew a stark, atavistic fear, primitive in its intensity.

Then Karen came in and the odd little incident was over. He smiled at her as he took the tray she was bearing and carried it across to a table by the shabby old sofa. In an instant he was Quinn again, infuriating, even frightening, certainly dangerous, but Quinn.

Karen poured tea, and accepted compliments on the scones with a charming grin, while Camilla gathered together what poise she had regained after the nasty rebuff of a few minutes before, and joined in the conversation. He left almost immediately, still coolly polite to Camilla.

That night as they ate dinner Karen said casually, 'John McLean asked me to the pictures tonight. They're showing *Gone With The Wind* again. Do you want to come?'

'And play gooseberry? Not on your life.'

Karen chuckled. 'It's not like that. He's a nice man, I like him, but he's a bit too serious for me.'

But she enjoyed her evening out, although she didn't say much about it over breakfast. The rain had eased enough for Camilla to go out to check the culvert without being drenched. There was not a sign of any movement in the metal or the rocks, so with a lighter heart she strode across to look over the in-calf heifers.

As she came back the clouds parted and a ray of sun leapt down, gilding the grass and the trees so that the raindrops glowed like golden particles. Camilla stopped, watching, her eyes suddenly filling with tears.

She had never been so confused, so astonished at herself. Quinn was working his way into her heart, filling all the empty areas with the warmth and power of his personality, and she was helpless against him. Was she unable to cope on her own? Did she have to have someone to love? Was she about to make the same mistake she had done with Dave?

But even as she wondered, she shook her head. No. Quinn's effect on her life was too potent. She had only to think of him and her senses were heightened, her emotions sharpened into acuteness. She wanted him; for the first time she admitted that she wanted to make love with him rather more than she wanted to breathe, yet she wanted to talk to him, to touch his mind and soul as he touched hers.

He was infinitely fascinating to her, the way he thought and felt just as mysterious and intriguing as the way he affected her senses, yet he was a man she could come to know. Some strange link had been forged between them.

He hated her working for Joe in the market gardens. She knew why. He was, she thought with a small smile, a very protective man. It was no longer fashionable for men to admit to those instincts, but she doubted that Quinn would ever change. He would be as fiercely protective of his children and his mother, of any woman. It was the way he was made, with an inborn urge to cherish.

Some women might find it smothering; perhaps it was a weakness in her that she should feel it to be infinitely endearing. Or perhaps, she thought with a cynical little smile, she needed a rest.

She didn't get one for the rest of the week, as the market garden was coming into full winter production, which meant vast numbers of cabbages and cauliflowers and broccoli to cut, and tomatoes and courgettes to pick in the tunnel houses. There at least, sheltered by the curved plastic walls and roof, it was warm. Outside it was cold, the sunny days afflicted with a cold southerly wind and quick, fierce showers.

'August weather,' she grumbled to Karen on Friday morning. 'I hate it in August and I hate it now.'

'Well, at least you don't have to milk the cows in it. I won't be home for dinner. I'm going to eat at the hotel with John.'

Camilla gave her a doubtful glance before essaying awkwardly, 'I hope you're not going to...' The words dried on her tongue.

'No, I'm not. I like him very much, but if he shows signs of becoming too enamoured I'll tell him that I'm not the sort of person he should be falling in love with.' Karen's voice was very steady.

'And why not?'

Her fierceness took Karen by surprise. She responded with a swift hug. 'You're terribly good for my ego, love. You know what I mean, though.'

'No, I don't. Why shouldn't you be the sort of person John should fall for? You had no doubts about Quinn!'

Karen gave her a calm, almost resigned look. 'Because with Quinn it wouldn't be love. He's more than capable of looking after himself, and what he'd have wanted from me would have been a short, wildly passionate affair with pleasant farewells when it was over. It would take more than me to hurt him—he's very self-contained. You can tell what sort of man he is; he likes women, but he doesn't let them get too close. John is—different.'

CHAPTER SEVEN

CAMILLA didn't see Quinn again for a week. Karen settled into her job as smoothly as if she had always worked in a small country town, and the weather turned thoroughly nasty in a dense, driving downpour that led to minor flooding and a couple of trees down in the shelter belts.

On the first fine day Camilla headed over to the boundary fence with a chainsaw. She was wielding it on an old hakea that had fallen from her place on to Falls when Quinn drove up in the Land Rover filled with larger dogs than he normally carried. As he got out of the cab he gave a curt word of command and they stayed obediently inside. Camilla switched off the chainsaw. Beside her, in the noisy silence, Ben began to growl softly.

'Quiet, Ben,' she said, straightening up. 'Those are pig dogs. They're too big for you.'

She removed her earmuffs, pushing a lock of hair back across her damp brow. In the manner of autumn, the weather was now beautiful, warm and mellow, the sun beating down with the force of summer. Succumbing to temptation, she had put on an old pair of shorts and a checked shirt with the sleeves rolled up.

Her eyes clung to Quinn as he came towards her. He too was wearing shorts: denim ones, faded and well-washed, that clung like a second skin. The boots he wore should have been incongruous, but taken in conjunction with the knife in a leather sheath across his lean hips, and the forbidding cast to his features, they made him look wild and dangerous.

'Are you going pig-hunting?' she asked.

He nodded. 'Damned boar's been coming out of the bush and killing the lambs.'

As did a growing number of sheep in the north, Quinn's ewes lambed in autumn, so the lambs were still small enough to be vulnerable to a predator like the boar.

Alarm edged her words. 'And you're going after it with only a knife?'

He lifted his brows, but said nothing about her unexpected concern, answering with a quick shake of his head, 'No, I've got a rifle. This is just in case any of the lambs are still alive.'

Sickened, she looked away. Dogs that slaughtered sheep indiscriminately, wild pigs in the hills that killed lambs—nature red in tooth and claw, she thought wearily.

'Leave this.' His voice was curt and commanding. 'I'll have someone clear it away by tonight.'

She responded to his tone with a flare of temper. 'I'm quite capable of doing it myself, thank you. The hakea was on my property.'

'And now most of it is on mine,' he said. 'Leave it.' Adding silkily. 'And don't sulk.'

Her head jerked around to scan his merciless profile, a sculpted slash against the green hill beyond. 'I am not sulking!'

'You're being childish. It will take one of my men much less time to do it.' And as she bristled he gave her a warm, coaxing smile. 'And then I won't have to worry about you hurting yourself.'

She fought the melting urge to yield with words that dripped ice. 'You're an arrogant, high-handed swine, and I am not the sort of woman who surrenders to a liberal dose of the famous Fraser charm. I don't like being manipulated.'

'No, you'd rather wallow in a set of hang-ups you acquired because you were ten inches taller than most of the boys in your class for most of your school life.' Steel showed nakedly through the contemptuous words.

For almost the first time in her life she knew what it was to lose control of her temper. 'How dare you discuss me with Karen? I won't listen to this feeble pop psychology!' she shouted.

'There's very little I don't dare to do,' he said, and actually laughed.

Her anger was so strong, she had to do something physical. Fingers curled into claws, she launched herself at him, her mouth tight and fierce and scarlet in the whiteness of her face.

Quinn grinned, his mouth a hard, mirthless line. Still furious, she swung her hand in a blow that he deflected with ease, before grabbing her hand to carry it to his mouth. Her fingers curled again as he bit her palm, and the mound under her thumb and the tip of her fore-finger, his teeth leaving small red marks on the skin. She gasped as lightning jagged through her at the touch of his mouth.

'I like you this way,' he said, his narrowed eyes brilliant as they searched her face. 'Your eyes gleam like crystals, bold and bright and sharp, and you look alive, as you were meant to look.'

His voice was silk and fur, deep and soft, winding its way through her nerves and bones and cells so that her body stirred with a sweet, wild ecstasy. Her tongue stole out to touch lips dry and hot with need; she blushed as his eyes followed the slight, alluring movement, nar-rowing into pin-points then widening suddenly, the pupils dilating so that the green was a thin rim around a depthless darkness.

In a voice that was husky and impeded she said, 'Angry?'

'No. You're not angry now. You look untamed, a little frightening, like a creature from a fantasy. The first time I saw you I wondered if the wildness was locked so far behind bars that it never escaped, and I wanted to know what you'd look like when it did. That's why you weren't popular at school, Camilla, because you are too much for most men, for young men. All that fire and passion, it makes demands, it's a threat...'

The words came from between lips that barely moved. Helplessly, her face dazed and waiting, she looked up into those eyes as his mouth came down on hers, softly and then brutally, like a primitive claim.

He kissed her as though she were his, joined body and soul in a bondage as old as time, as strong as iron, as untamed as fire. It was like nothing that had ever happened to her, not even when he had kissed her before. Her body arched, fierce as winter, bold as summer, and her hands pulled him down while her tongue mated fiercely, angrily, with his.

And then she was free, and he was looking at her, the planes and angles of his face accentuated and dominant. 'You don't need careful handling,' he said quietly. 'You need to find yourself. And when you've done that, God help us all.'

Her hand moved up to touch her bruised mouth, then stroked along the clean curves of his. Her fingers, she noted with a strange detachment, were trembling. Beneath the soft, sensitive pads his mouth burned; she jerked away as if stung, and he smiled.

'I'm sorry I was rude to you the other day,' he said. 'I was angry. You have no idea how infuriating you are when you give me that patrician look down your nose.'

Her world had just fallen around her in fire and convulsions, and he could speak with that infuriating note of teasing in his voice!

She was afraid, because she didn't know what to do. She thought wildly that she didn't even know whether she was the same person any more. His kisses seemed to strip her character away, revealing a new woman, one who burned with desire and anger, who lived at a faster, fiercer pace, a woman with needs so strong that the only safe thing to do was banish them behind barricades that she had spent a lifetime building.

She thought of her mother, and wondered desperately if she had felt like this about the man she had married. Had Karen about any of her lovers? Was Quinn's searing possession of her faculties and desires normal? If so, how had Karen managed to survive being in love so often? Would this too fade, and die, as Karen's love-affairs did?

The thought was a lance of pain through her heart. The sun hid behind a cloud and shadows chased each other across the green countryside. She was wrenched by a melancholy so profound that unbidden tears ached at the back of her eyes. Thoughts warred in her mind, must have been reflected in her countenance, because he asked, 'What's the matter?'

His voice was wonderfully gentle, and she blinked. 'Nothing.'

'Then why are you looking like a wanderer who knows there's no way home?'

His perception shouldn't have surprised her. Sometimes he knew her better than she did herself.

In a husky little voice she replied, 'I'm just—confused.' And was angry, because of course he would laugh at her, or want to know why.

Instead he said gently, 'Yes, I know. Unfortunately, I can't help you. You have to be the one to make the decisions, to come to some conclusions.'

'I don't know what you want from me,' she cried out, obscurely angered by his understanding. It would have been more satisfying if he'd been his usual autocratic self. She could have resisted, or allowed herself to be swept along by his authority; at least she would have had something to fight.

He laughed. 'That's easy enough. I want all of you. But not until you're ready to give it. I refuse to allow you to embark on something you don't fully accept or understand. I want an adult as a lover, not a grieving girl who falls headlong into decisons and spends the rest of her life feeling guilty and inadequate because they don't work out the way she hoped.'

Well. That was plain enough. He wanted a lover strong enough to take responsibility for her own life, and absolve him of any. The typical male fantasy.

Camilla was wounded and furious, but caution made her restrain the searing emotions that boiled deep inside. 'Thank you,' she said colourlessly. 'And when it's over, presumably I should be able to say goodbye without any messy, undignified hysterics, unlike the woman I found crying in the calf paddock just after we came up north.'

She had hit a nerve. His mouth tightened, but he said evenly, 'Why anticipate the end now? As for Carole, she knew from the start that there was no possibility of marriage, and as soon as I realised that she was hatching plans I broke it off as gently as I could.'

'Why? She was beautiful and elegant, she knew how to behave, and surely you want a son to leave Falls to?'

He said calmly, 'That's none of your business.'

'But why?' she persisted, knowing that she was treading on very thin ground, but impelled by some violent need to hit out at him. 'Was she lousy in bed?'

He punished her for the vulgar question by saying, 'No, she was very good in bed. Generous and loving and sensuous—the ideal mistress. And if I ever hear that repeated, I'll see that you suffer for it. I don't want to discuss her any further, Camilla.'

She subsided, more than a little horrified by her insolent audacity.

After a moment he went on, still in that lethally even voice, 'And yes, I do want children. Do you?'

'Yes, eventually,' she said in muted tones. 'Several. I was an only child, and it wasn't a good thing to be. But so were you, weren't you?'

'Yes. Like you, I'd rather have several.'

It hurt to think of a woman bearing his children. She thought savagely that she was becoming stupidly possessive about a man who refused to accept bonds or links, who had neatly avoided promising her any permanence in the relationship that he was doing his best to initiate.

He interrupted her resentful thoughts by saying, 'Leave the tree for the men to cut up, Camilla.'

When she said nothing, merely stood looking at him from opaque eyes, he said quietly, 'Please. I can't stop and help you.'

She said, 'I can do it.'

'I know you can. I'd rather you didn't.'

Her mouth twisted. 'All right.'

He watched her for a moment, as though judging the value of her surrender, then nodded. 'I'll see you later.'

A little touched by his care, she essayed a cautious smile. It proved to be a mistake, because he construed it as an invitation and bent and kissed her thoroughly, taking his time about it as he held her against the hard length of his body.

Camilla sighed voluptuously into his mouth, and he kissed her again, his quickening body convincing her at last to pull away. He grinned, flicked her cheek with a casual finger and left.

There had been complete confidence in that smile, a kind of open masculine satisfaction which warned her that he was convinced of her ultimate surrender.

Unfortunately, his confidence was echoed by hers. Sooner or later she was going to give him what he wanted on his own insulting terms, because her body was slowly becoming sensitised to his. What had started out as a wildfire attraction was rapidly becoming something stronger and more dangerous. She was becoming obsessed with him.

When the Land Rover with its cargo of rifle and pig dogs had gone she stashed the saw on the back of the tractor and drove back to the house, fighting an uneasy feeling that she had been manipulated. An hour later, as she worked on the neglected garden around the house, she grimaced at the noisy chatter of a distant chainsaw. Even later, she wasn't surprised by a call from Mrs Fraser.

'The men brought back a great load of hakea wood,' she said. 'Do you want it, Camilla? I know it's not terribly good firewood, but it's better than nothing.'

'Yes, I'll——'

'They'll bring it down on the truck.'

'Thank you. Did Quinn get the boar he was hunting?'

'No, he didn't expect to. They lie up during the day, you know. He's going out tonight with a couple of the others, and with any luck they'll track it down then. Awful things! If they'd stay in the bush no one would mind, but they kill so many lambs, quite wantonly, be-

cause they don't eat them all. Now, before I forget, dear,
I have some yoghurt here to get you started. I'll bring
it down tomorrow.'

'No, no, I'll come up, you don't need to come down.'

'It will be no problem, I assure you.'

They chatted for a few moments on inconsequential
things. After she'd hung up, Camilla made a cup of tea
and was just settling down to enjoy it when the phone
went again. This time it was Karen.

'I won't be home at the usual time,' she said cheerfully. 'John and I are going over to Port Arthur for
dinner. He hasn't got the time to come and collect me,
and I'm not borrowing that heap of yours, so I'll shower
at his place and wear what I've got on.'

Camilla said, 'I resent that aspersion on my trusty vehicle, but I think you're wise. You always look stunning,
and Port Arthur is not quite as sophisticated as
Auckland, especially at this time of the year. Have fun.'

Very flippantly, Karen said, 'I always do, thank you
very much.'

Camilla drank her tea with a smile curling her mouth.
Karen might have given up on her stated intention of
pursuing Quinn, but she was going to enjoy herself while
she explored the quieter charms of the vet.

When the truck arrived she went out to help stack the
neatly sawn logs in the woodshed, and after that it was
too late to begin any serious work, so she found herself
in the rare position of having some time on her hands.
She checked the cows, tied Ben up and fed him, then
went in shivering, for a cruel little wind had sprung up.
It was too early to put on dinner so she ran herself a
deep bath, locked the doors, and took one of Karen's
magazines as well as the latest dairy bulletin in with her.

An hour later she stepped out of the tub. One of the
first things Karen had bought with her pay-cheque was

a large mirror which she had hung in the bathroom, that being, she had declared, the only room in the house with decent enough lighting for her to put on her make-up.

Camilla was still not accustomed to it, flinching every time she caught sight of herself because for a milli-second she thought that someone else had wandered into the room, but now the towel slowed and stilled. She peered at the dim outlines of her body through the steam on the glass. On an impulse she wiped the mirror and stood looking at her reflection.

Even flushed with immersion in the water she was pale, she thought dispassionately. Pale, soft skin, so trans-parent in parts that veins made faint shadows beneath the whiteness. Long, long legs, narrow hips, a boyish waist and small white breasts, rose-tipped; she surveyed them gravely, thinking that they looked barely adequate for the job of nursing. Embarrassed by her scrutiny, she turned and looked over her shoulder at her image. Her shoulders were wide, her backside neat and more mus-cular than most women's, as were her arms and legs.

With the best will in the world, she decided despair-ingly, she could not be described as seductive. Add an unpretty face with slanted, colourless eyes and dead-straight black hair cut in her best approximation of an urchin, and what was there for a man like Quinn to want?

Nothing. Which meant that it must be the farm.

And yet ... when he kissed her ...

Liquid heat suffused her body. Hastily she swung around, snatching up the towel, and to her astonishment her breasts peaked. She watched them in the mirror, the small nipples contracting, tightening into buds. The sen-sation was almost painful, yet so fleeting, so exquisite.

'No!' Her voice was panic-stricken. She dragged the towel over herself and huddled into her nightgown and dressing-gown, as though by covering her treacherous body she could hide from the sensations curling through it.

She had just lit the fire in the dining-room when there was a knock at the door. Hastily, her body still smarting with unresolved need, she asked, 'Who is it?'

'Quinn.'

'I...' She had been going to demand that he wait, but it would be cold on the back porch. A quick glance through the window revealed that it was also pitch-dark. For a moment she hesitated, as panic-stricken as though he were a hunter and she the helpless prey, then she went across and unlocked the door.

He came into the room, big, smelling faintly of the rain she could hear falling softly on the corrugated-iron roof, and stood looking down at her with a faint smile curving his mouth. Dressed in superbly cut trousers and a fine wool shirt, a jar in his hand, he looked like the men in Karen's glossy magazine, only infinitely more powerful and imposing.

'My mother has sent you down a starter kit for yoghurt,' he said gravely, handing over the jar. 'I'd be careful if I were you—it looks feral to me.'

'Oh—it's not. How kind of her,' she babbled. 'You didn't need to bring it down tonight. Thank you so much—I'll just go and get into some clothes.'

'You don't need to run away. I won't throw you on the floor and make violent, passionate love to you,' he said, wicked laughter creasing the skin around his eyes as she took an involuntary step backwards. 'I rather like you like that. You look like a little girl, scrubbed and ready for bed.'

'I'd feel happier in clothes,' she said grittily. 'Come into the sitting-room.'

Why did she want to shunt him into the sitting-room, which was tidy but cold?

Mouth firming sardonically, he looked down at the flames of the fire. 'I'll wait here.'

'Would you like something to drink?' she asked in her politest voice, wishing that she was wearing anything other than the dark blue dressing-gown that had definitely seen better days.

His smile teased. 'No.'

She fled to the sound of his laughter. As she pulled on a skirt and blouse, she vowed never again to succumb to the temptation to have a bath at any other time than just before bed. She was prickly and defiant when she came back into the room, but he got up from her chair and smiled at her with such charm that she felt all of her irritation seep away. When she smiled back at him a little flame at the back of his eyes made her hurry into speech.

'Did you see any signs of the boar?'

That betraying glitter didn't fade, although his voice was mocking. 'Yes, but not enough to follow him. He'd gone to ground. I'll go out again tomorrow morning.'

'Be careful,' she said automatically, thinking of his mother's strictures about his recklessness. Wild boars were cunning and fierce, and had been known to kill with their huge tusks.

'I have every intention of being very careful. I have a lot to live for.'

'How many lambs did you lose?'

The lights in his eyes became a hard sheen. 'Twenty, damn him.'

She grimaced. 'Bad luck.'

'Bad management. Never mind, they'll be the last ones I lose to that old devil.'

The note of grim purpose in his voice made her skin go cold. At that moment she almost felt sorry for the boar. However, she said, 'Sit down, do.'

'Try your telephone first,' he suggested. 'I rang to let you know I was coming, but it appears to be dead.'

She frowned, but went across and lifted the receiver, to be greeted by the clicks and hisses that indicated it was definitely unusable. The telephone line was vulnerable, any storm likely to see it broken by branches driven by the wind. Still, if the last blow had damaged it she would have expected the break to have occurred then, not now when all was still.

'Oh, it's so maddening,' she muttered. 'It must have only just happened. I was talking on it not that long ago.' She sank back down in the chair, saying with an attempt at lightness, 'I'll get Karen to phone Faults tomorrow from the boutique.'

'You do that.' He waited until she was settled before shocking her by asking, 'Did you get what you wanted from the bank manager the other day?'

So he had heard Karen's query. 'It's no business of yours,' she said rather hopelessly, because it was quite clear that he had made it his concern.

He said in the soft, menacing voice she hated, 'Don't be a fool, Camilla.'

Childishly she retorted, 'No one asked you to busy yourself with my affairs! You have no right to interfere!'

'No rights that you'll grant me,' he returned, 'but I'd be a poor sort of neighbour if I didn't make a push to help someone who's struggling, wouldn't I? Especially when it's someone I care about.'

Put like that, of course, it would be sheer churlishness to object. She gave him a long level look, and saw amusement and another quality in the striking face; a determination so steely and sharp that she knew she would smash herself to pieces if she tried to withstand it.

More than anything some weak, craven part of her wanted to give in to his will, surrender and let him take over her life as he seemed intent on doing. That was where the danger lay.

Summoning her resolve, she said angrily, 'Even good neighbours keep out of each other's financial affairs. Why, Quinn? Why are you doing this?'

He didn't pretend not to know what she was asking. 'Because you have too much against you. You're brave, and valiant, and too bloody loyal, fighting valiantly for Dave's dreams, Dave's needs. But determination isn't enough. I've seen it happen before, the vicious cycle of lack of capital; however hard you struggle, you'll never get out of the mire, unless it's by a miracle. And when you finally have to admit defeat, you'll have lost everything—youth, laughter, hope and love—and you'll be left broken in the ruins of those dreams. If I thought you were going to be able to win through I'd stand back and let you go——'

She said indignantly, because he was only saying what she knew to be the truth, the truth which she had tried to hide from, 'You have no say in the matter!'

'You deserve to win,' he said, shrugging. 'No one could doubt your hard work, but I'm afraid it's a tough world, and you started with too many strikes against you. I've given you a year to sort yourself out, but you haven't done the sensible thing so I've decided to do it for you. You can kick and struggle and complain all you like, but from now on, my obstinate, courageous little love, you are going to do what is good for you.'

Shaken to the core by the careless endearment, she managed to ignore it and toss back a sour comment. 'You mean what you think is good for me!'

'Exactly.'

He smiled across at her flushed, indignant face, and leaned over to anchor her to the chair with his hand on her wrist. His eyes fell to the pale fragility of it, encompassed by the dark strength of his hand. Camilla followed his gaze, finding it unexpectedly erotic. Her tongue dampened her lip, was withdrawn hastily.

He said deeply, 'You are surprisingly strong, but I am stronger. And I'll use any advantage I have, so why don't you just accept it?'

Tiny nerve impulses were fleeting from her wrist to her breasts, and from there to other susceptible parts of her body. She shifted uneasily in the chair, dragging her eyes away from her imprisoned wrist, but to her horror she felt the tight drawing sensation in her nipples, and knew that beneath her shirt the little tips were budding. She thought desperately that she could feel the material dragging across them, almost painful and yet an incitement.

A quick look showed that he was smiling, the corners of his well-cut mouth pulling in to make a surprisingly sensuous outline. His eyes were clear, blazing green, crystalline and intense. She knew that hers would be the same, their lack of colour emphasising the expanding iris.

Desperately, buying time in the only way that came to her mind, she asked, 'Why did Uncle Philip hate you so much? You have never told me what you did that caused all the trouble.'

Reluctantly, he let her hand go, his own resting on the arm of the chair. She watched beneath her lashes as the long fingers clenched into a fist, then relaxed.

'Very well,' he said, after a tense pause, 'although it doesn't show either of us in a very good light. Your uncle was as obstinate and cross-grained a man as any I've ever met, and at the time it all started I was young and sewing my wild oats.'

Relieved that she had averted whatever had been going to happen, she allowed herself an ironic smile.

He countered it with a straight, hard look. 'My father had just died and I had to come back from an immensely enjoyable sojourn on a big station in Queensland to take over Falls. They were doing interesting things with cattle, breeding them carefully for drought and tick resistance, and when I came away I bought a bull from the station. He was extremely expensive, but he was worth it. For years Philip had been a damned nuisance, refusing to do his share of keeping up the boundary fence, refusing to keep the place clear of thistles, behaving as if he were still farming at the end of the last century. He didn't believe in anything new-fangled, so he had to be forced to TB-test his cattle, and when brucellosis testing was not compulsory he refused to have it done.'

Camilla sighed. 'My mother said he was an obstinate man.'

'I'm all for people indulging their idiosyncrasies,' he said with cold irony, 'provided they don't hurt anyone else. Unfortunately, Philip thought I was an arrogant young upstart who needed to be taught a lesson or two. He may have been right. When my bull arrived he not only scoffed at my reasons for buying it, he bought in some cattle that hadn't been tested for buscellosis, and with criminal carelessness let them through the boundary.'

Camilla winced. He nodded. 'Yes. One developed brucellosis, so some of mine, including the bull, had to be destroyed. Fortunately I'd been keeping him quarantined, so I was able to contain any more infection. But I lost my temper. Philip and I had an argument, and I called him names that anyone would have found hard to forgive. When I came to my senses he made it obvious that, as far as he was concerned, that was it. From then on he did whatever he could to make life difficult for me.'

'He knew he was in the wrong, so he found it impossible to forgive.' She nodded. 'People are strange, aren't they?'

'You seem to understand your uncle,' he said coolly. 'Perhaps you should try to use some of that perception on me. Then you might be able to convince yourself that I don't intend to use the fact that you want to go to bed with me as a lever to steal your inheritance away.'

Colour burned across her skin. Sickened by her own weakness in not telling him before, she said sharply, 'You can't. According to Uncle Philip's will, if I sell to you the proceeds are divided up and dispatched to three charities, and I'd be left to pay off the mortgage. I'd be bankrupt.'

He looked at her as though he didn't believe it. 'He did what?' A moment's incredulous silence, then he said dangerously, 'And Dave went into debt, knowing that——'

'He didn't know he was going to die,' she interrupted, half appalled that she had finally told him. Now, she thought, if he goes now, I'll know that he only wanted the farm. 'He thought we'd have plenty of time to pay off the bank.'

His hand clenched. 'He knew this place was never going to be an economic dairy unit. He asked the local farm advisory officer, then ignored all the advice he was given and borrowed on a rising market, only it was the interest rates that went up, not the butterfat prices!'

'If he disregarded advice, then surely the bank is just as culpable? It lent him the money.'

He said between his teeth. 'The bank is in the business of lending money. Presumably they assumed that if he came a cropper I'd buy the place and they'd get their money back. Everyone in the district knows that I want it. But I'll bet no one knows about that caveat in Philip's will, especially not the bank manager.'

She winced and shrank back, because he was so cold, so angry. When he looked at her his eyes were impersonal, icy with rage, and she knew that Philip had been right, he had only wanted the farm. What she was seeing was frustration because now he knew that he was never going to get it.

Tonelessly, she said, 'I think you'd better go.'

He scanned her rigid face, then the wide shoulders lifted in a brief shrug. 'All right.'

Half an hour later she was still in the chair, staring at the dying fire. She had never known that pain could be so intense that it hurt to breathe, hurt even to think. Huddled into the shabby upholstery, she was trying to stop her brain from going around and around in agonisingly futile repining when she heard Ben giving tongue.

Slightly alarmed, because there seemed more tension in the barking than usual, she checked the locked door, then switched the light off before moving over to the window. She was not normally jumpy, but the scene with Quinn had thrown her whole nervous system out of order and she felt as though she were teetering on a knife-edge.

In a way she almost welcomed the alarm. It took her mind off the pain that gnawed at her heart. Outside it was very dark; she could see the lights of Falls homestead through the trees, but nothing else. The cloud pall that hung heavily over the earth probably made Ben's barks echo, emphasising them, she decided, listening with strained ears for any other noise.

After a few seconds he settled down and she walked into the bedroom, but before she had time to switch on the light he began again, deep, threatening barks interspersed with higher, anxious yelps and whines. Frowning, she stood very still in the tense darkness, but she could hear nothing above the thunder of her heart.

The barking died away, but in its place came a low rumble of growls, infinitely menacing. Camilla's hand stole to between her breasts, clenching. She knew the noise he made when he scented one of the night creatures, and this was not it.

From the window she peered out into the smothering blackness. She could see no movement, but through the growls the rattle of the dog's chain revealed that he was racing about. A crescendo, almost a frenzy, of noise erupted and she realised that he was flinging himself at the end of his chain, trying to get at whatever threatened him.

Fear prickled through her veins like ice, robbing her of will. A cowardly portion of her brain suggested that she ring Quinn, but hard on its heels was the fact that now, when she needed it, the phone line was out. She drew a deep breath, forcing the stupid, useless panic back, and made up her mind. In the corner of the wardrobe was Dave's shotgun. Tiptoeing across, she groped for it, pulling it out. She knew what to do; even in the dark she could manage to fit two shells into the breech. Very quietly she went back to the window and eased it open, calling out, 'Quiet, Ben! Stop it!'

There was a momentary silence, then Ben began again, letting off a fusillade of furious barks. Whatever threatened him was still there. Taking a deep breath, she thumbed the safety-catch and fired through the open window into the sky. Ben howled and shot back into the kennel, and through the ringing in her ears she heard footsteps thudding rapidly across the paddock towards the road. A few seconds later, a darkened car started up and sped away towards the main road.

It had just got beyond the entrance to Falls when another car came rocketing down the drive and headed up towards her gate. Quinn, she thought, shaking with a sick reaction as she yanked the window shut and forced herself to walk back into the kitchen.

Sure enough, it was he. As he came up the path in a silent rush he called her name, and, almost sobbing with reaction, she opened the door. He took one look at the gun in her hand, and demanded sharply, 'What the hell——? Are you all right?'

CHAPTER EIGHT

'YES.' Camilla bent the barrels and shucked out the cartridge, put the shotgun on the floor then sat limply down on the nearest chair. 'Somebody was prowling about—he left his car on the road but he's gone now.'

'You didn't see who it was?' Quinn's voice was flat and lethal.

'No.' She swallowed. 'I didn't see him at all. Ben was going berserk, so I knew something was there.'

He went across to the telephone and tried it, then turned, his expression coldly controlled. 'Damn, I'd forgotten it was out of order. Wait here and I'll have a look outside.'

'I'll come with you,' she said promptly. 'Do you want the gun?'

'No. If you'd feel safer with it, bring it. Carry it broken, and if by some remote chance there is someone still around, be damned careful with it!'

Almost immediately they found footsteps in the mud by the garage. The intruder had come quietly across the paddocks and stood for some time by the corner, apparently not rousing Ben until he stepped out from the lee of the building and began to move towards the house.

'He must have waited here until I left,' Quinn said in a quiet, deadly tone. 'He stood for quite some time, the marks are obscured where he shuffled.'

Camilla had to clench her teeth to stop them from chattering. 'I wonder what he wanted.'

'I don't know. I'll take you home to Falls and ring the police from there.'

She could think of nothing more desirable; the house and farm seemed suddenly alien, antagonistic. However, 'Karen will be coming home soon,' she objected.

'She can stay with us for the night, too.'

He looked up sharply as the sound of an engine broke into the night, but it was another car coming down the station drive. In it were three of the men from Falls, all roused by the sound of the shot, all concerned when they saw the footprints in the mud.

'Head off and see if there are any tyre marks on the road,' Quinn told the driver. 'I'd like someone to stay here and bring Karen up to the homestead.'

Another set of lights came up the road. 'This should be her,' Camilla said.

Instead, it was Joe from the market garden. He had heard the shot and come to see what was going on, but almost immediately John McLean's car followed, and a shaken Karen agreed immediately to go to the homestead. John took them, leaving them with an alarmed Mrs Fraser while he went back.

'I'll get you a brandy,' the older woman said after a sharp look at Camilla.

She began to object, but subsided. Now that it was all over, a brandy seemed eminently desirable.

The last drops were trickling heatedly down her throat when Quinn arrived back. Searching his face, Camilla set the glass down. 'Did you find anything more?'

'No. He's not likely to come back.' A menacing amusement glimmered behind his lashes. 'I imagine you scared the hell out of him when you fired the gun. He's probably still running.'

'I didn't know what else to do.' She shivered. 'I certainly didn't expect to wake up half the neighbourhood.'

'Oh, we look after our own.' He let that sink in, then resumed, 'There's been a spate of stealing from various farms around the district, so probably our man was on the look-out for anything he could pick up. You won't see any more of him.'

Indeed, in the broad light of day, the whole incident seemed more farcical than frightening. Camilla woke in a pretty guest-room that overlooked the serene gardens at the back of the house, and lay for a long moment wondering where she was. Then, instead of thinking of the prowler, she found herself remembering the moment when she'd told Quinn of the condition in Philip's will, and he had walked out of the door.

Pain was cold, an icy cloak stealing over her, shutting her away from warmth and love and laughter. She thought that she had never really been happy; perhaps her mother's melancholy, so deeply rooted that it had become part of her personality, had infected Camilla with the conviction that all happiness was fleeting, and the greater the joy, the higher the price exacted.

Perhaps that was why she had married Dave. In some hidden part of her she had realised that he could never touch her deepest emotions, and therefore she would be safe with him. Her thoughts angered and dismayed her. Agitatedly she got out of bed and walked across the muted crimsons and blues of an Oriental carpet to lean out of the window so that she could see out across the smiling hills, green and lush, rising into purple heights where the immutable bush dreamed under a canopy of blue.

But it was impossible to hide from her thoughts. Relentlessly, painfully, they nagged away all her pleasure at the view. Her mother had been right. She had been right. Deeply as she had grieved for Dave, it was nothing compared to the agony that racked her now. How had she been so stupid? She had allowed Quinn to become so important that his betrayal cut through her like knives of pain.

Her aching eyes scanned the blue and gold morning outside. It was useless to tell herself that he had said nothing about love, nothing about commitment. He had not lied to her, had not tried to persuade her with false promises. No, she had done that herself. Wistfully she wondered if love was ever worth it. She was going through exactly the same pangs that had affected Quinn's mistress so long ago, and for exactly the same reason: because he had rejected her.

Had Dave felt like this when he'd realised that she couldn't love him? Her heart faltered as she wondered if it had been disillusionment that had made him so careless of his life that he couldn't see the point in fitting a canopy to the tractor.

A knock on the door stopped her reverie. It was just as well; she was becoming maudlin with self-pity and guilt.

It was Karen, sleekly dressed for work in the clothes she had brought from the house the night before. 'I thought I'd better remind you that breakfast is at seven-thirty,' she said as she came in. 'You didn't seem to be taking much in last night.'

Camilla gave her a wan smile. 'That brandy was not exactly conducive to thought.' It had ensured her a night's sleep, though.

'Just as well, you poor old thing. It must have been a horrifying experience. Thank goodness Ben takes his job so seriously.'

Camilla shuddered. 'It wasn't much fun.'

'Such masterly understatement! It must have been terrifying. This place is absolutely magnificent, isn't it? I love the way they've decorated the bedrooms with a mixture of antique and really good modern furniture. I wonder what it would be like to have so much money? I suppose if you've grown up with this sort of background, it explains a lot—that calm, arrogant confidence, for starters. Although, when I come to think of it, I've met other men who were loaded and they weren't anywhere near such magnificent beasts. An alpha male, that's what Quinn is. I think he'd have got to the top if he'd been born with nothing.'

Camilla, who emphatically agreed but could not bring herself to talk about him, nodded and said quietly, 'If I'm going to be ready on time I'd better get dressed.'

She would have given her soul to be able to avoid facing him, but she could think of no way out that wasn't both rude and cowardly. And, although she didn't mind being rude to Quinn, her battle was not with his mother.

So she washed her face and combed her hair and cleaned her teeth, practised a cool, unimpressed smile in the mirror, and dressed. Then she made her way down the staircase and went along to the morning-room next to the kitchen, her nerves so tense that she thought she might break into small pieces if anyone looked sideways at her.

But it wasn't too bad. Her heart gave a funny jump when he smiled at her and asked her how she had slept, but the very ordinariness of eating toast and marmalade and drinking coffee helped her cope. And if her eyes were kept severely away from the handsome face of the man who so effortlessly dominated the room, no one else seemed to notice.

After the meal he said calmly, 'Can you wait a moment, Camilla? I want to discuss a few things with you.'

Karen frowned. 'Will you be taking her back, Quinn, just in case there's anyone lying in wait?'

'Yes, but no one is.' Quinn's voice was infinitely reassuring. 'The house has been watched, just in case, but
there hasn't been a sign of anyone near it.'

'I can look after myself,' Camilla said indignantly.

'We know.' His tone was very dry. Once in the office,
he waited until she had been seated before asking, 'Do
you want to stay here for a few days?'

'No.' The answer was made without thought.

His mouth curled in an unpleasant smile. 'Hardly
flattering.'

She lifted her chin. 'I'm sorry, I didn't mean it like
that. If I stay here it's merely putting off the time I go
back, and I think it's better done sooner than later.'

'You won't be afraid?'

She shrugged. 'No. Only a stupid man would come
back after he'd had a shotgun fired at him.'

'I would say so.' His voice was so dry that she looked
up, and immediately wished she hadn't, because he was
watching her with that stabbing scrutiny that she found
so uncomfortable to parry.

Then he spoke about the real reason for taking her
into the office. 'Have you ever sat down and thought
hard about what you really want to do with your life?
Not Dave's plans, or your mother's hopes, but what you
would be happiest doing?'

She hid her disappointment with a shrug. 'I'm perfectly happy now.'

His eyes darkened and she saw the corners of his
mouth tighten. Good, she thought recklessly. But his
voice was even as he pursued, 'I won't believe that. That
you're happy farming, yes. But that you enjoy worrying
over every cent, working for Joe in the rain and the cold
because you need the money, wearing the same clothes
year after year——'

'I don't have to listen to this!' she flared, leaping to her feet.

He caught her by the upper arm, holding her still. His face was dark with angry colour, and he spoke between his teeth. 'Just for once, damn you, you're going to face exactly what you're doing to yourself. You're twenty-two and you live like a peasant in a Third World country.'

Shaking with a mixture of fear and rage, she spat, 'I told you, I can't sell the place!'

'You can lease it.'

'Not to you.' She pulled away, but, although he wasn't hurting her, she was held still. 'I have to work it. I can't let it be used by anyone else. Especially not you.'

Incredulously, he asked, 'You mean Philip more or less tied you to the place? Like a serf?'

She bit her lip, all of her anger draining from her. 'I— he said he didn't want it to go downhill.'

He said in total disgust, 'He wanted to make damned sure I never got my hands on it. All right, have you ever thought of contesting the will?'

There was no way she could free herself without an undignified struggle. 'I can't afford to,' she said numbly. Tears sparkled like colourless jewels in her eyes. 'I can't do anything,' she cried, for the first time accepting her real emotions. 'I'm trapped. If I sell the cows I could put beef cattle on the place, but they'd cost more than I could afford, and I wouldn't get enough back from them to pay the interest, let alone the actual loan. Dairying is the only way I can keep going.'

'All right,' he said slowly. His other hand came up and pulled her into the warmth of his body. 'Hush,' he whispered, stroking the damp wisps of hair off her brow. 'It's all right, we'll come up with something. Can I have a copy of that will?'

She stiffened, and he swore and held her away, his eyes stabbing into her pale face. He said savagely, 'I've tried, God knows, and you still think that all I want from you is the damned farm.'

Through pale lips she said, 'You left last night as soon as I told you I couldn't sell.'

'Yes. You were primed for a fight, and quite frankly, Camilla, I'm tired of quarrelling with you. I thought the best thing to do was let you calm down.' He paused, watching the smooth, closed contours of her face, then went on harshly, 'Besides, I had to get out. I couldn't forget how you looked when you opened the door, and it was getting harder by the minute to be as pragmatic and platonic as you obviously want me to be. And if we'd quarrelled—well, you make me so angry that I can barely think, and once I've lost control it's not only my temper that's easily roused.'

Camilla felt the heat surge across her skin, but defied it with a lifted chin and a level gaze. She could not allow the effect of his suddenly thickened voice to blind her to the truth. 'You want the farm,' she said, stating the obvious.

His face hardened. 'Yes, I want the farm.'

'Then that's all that counts, isn't it?'

She turned to go, but he used his hold on her arm to pull her close into his body, and once more she was a prisoner of the elemental attraction that made a fool of her will and her autonomy, sinking her so deeply in passion that instead of resisting she lifted her face in mute invitation, her eyelids drooping in a seductive, totally unconscious surrender.

But instead of kissing her, washing away all of her fears and inhibitions in the magic of his sensuality, he asked in a cold, flat voice, 'What sort of woman are you, Camilla?'

Her lashes flew up. A painful flood of colour heated the skin over her whole body.

Remorselessly, his eyes opaque as glacier ice, he said, 'You distrust me completely, yet I only have to touch you and you yield everything without a fight. If I am a complete opportunist, what sort of woman are you? One so at the mercy of her needs——'

The insult was stopped by her palm, cracking with involuntary speed across his mouth. Camilla stared at him, and the red mark on his skin, and her skin crawled. Not even last night had she been so afraid. But that he should think of her in exactly the same way as the driver of the truck made her lose any semblance of reason.

In a trembling voice she cried, 'How dare you insinuate——? You're exactly the same as all the rest! Everything, your protested concern, your kindness—"we look after our own",' she mimicked in savage mockery, 'it means nothing, because you think I'm eager to trade my self-respect for a little human warmth and comfort!'

'Comfort?' He almost threw her away from him, watching with eyes that flamed as she staggered and caught the edge of the desk to support herself. 'I've had damned little comfort, damned little warmth from you. I don't think you're capable of giving it. No wonder Dave tried to work himself into the grave! Very well, go back and worry yourself into a nervous breakdown or whatever it is you're headed for, and when you've exhausted every other option, come and ask me to help you then. I'm through with offering. Next time you're going to have to beg, and if I'm feeling in a good mood I might agree. Get out.'

Mrs Fraser insisted on accompanying her home. Numb, unable to accept what had happened, Camilla accepted her company listlessly. Had she misjudged Quinn? The emotions that had darkened his face to a bronzed, primeval mask of fury seemed entirely too convincing to be assumed. Of course, he wanted the farm, but such a violent reaction to the fact that he was never going to be able to get it would mean that he was a man in the grip of an obsession, and he was too well balanced for that.

If he had really wanted to help her, she had insulted him for the last time. Remembering the disdain that had hardened his expression as he'd ordered her contemptuously out of the office and his life, her heart shuddered. Perhaps all of her self-doubts were correct; she wasn't able to love. But if this wasn't love, this hunger that burned through her with a painful ecstasy, then what was it?

Quinn rang late in the afternoon. Her foolish heart leapt into her throat, but all that he said, after a perfunctory greeting, was, 'I rang the quarry manager and he told me that the driver he sacked left the district almost immediately after he was given the boot.'

'Oh.' Surprisingly enough, it hadn't occurred to her that the man might be the intruder. Tonelessly, she said, 'Thank you.'

'Think nothing of it. I'm glad your phone is back on,' he said with deadly courtesy, and hung up.

She turned away, blinking, her hopes lying cold and inert in her breast.

That night she let Ben sleep on the back porch, untied for once, but no further intruder marred the stillness of the night, and if Camilla had been feeling normal she would have been completely reassured. As it was, she lay awake all night, her mind worrying over the quarrel, each bitter word he had said etching itself into her brain in letters of ice, dull and cold and as frozen as her emotions. Morning dawned clear and still, but with ominous

knotted wisps of cloud in the sky that denoted a change
in the weather. Appropriate, she thought bleakly.

During breakfast John McLean rang. When Karen
came back to the table Camilla asked, 'And where are
you going tonight?'

Karen's voice was elaborately careless. 'Oh, I've decided to stay home.'

Camilla put her piece of toast down. 'Why?'

'I'm tired.'

'Have you and John had an argument?' Camilla asked
tentatively.

'No. Surely I can be a little tired? I'm not Super-
woman, you know.'

Camilla lifted her brows. Karen being innocently
righteous was quite a sight. 'Don't be an idiot. The intruder is not going to come back, not now he knows I'm
likely to fill him full of shotgun pellets.'

'Have you ever wondered if it was that creep who
brought the load of metal?'

'Actually I hadn't, but Quinn rang to say that he'd
left the district as soon as he was sacked. Anyway,' she
pointed out reasonably, 'he wasn't given the boot because of me, he'd been reported for getting too stroppy
with someone else.'

'I know, but men like that...' Karen frowned. 'Still,
I suppose if he's left——'

'Look, there have always been pilferers around; it's a
fact of life. Bales of wool disappear from woolsheds,
rustlers drive up in trucks and load them with prime beef
or sheep, orchardists and market gardeners lose sprays
and equipment. It's not a common occurrence, but it
does happen, and the people who do it are thieves, not
rapists or murderers. Now that whoever it was knows
that Ben and I are on the alert, he won't be coming back.'

Karen allowed herself to be convinced, and after ringing John to accept his invitation went off to work. Drinking the rest of her tea, Camilla wondered if this time her cousin had actually found someone she loved. Karen was very reticent about John; she rarely mentioned his name, and never said anything about her feelings for him, but lately she seemed to walk in a lovely glow.

Camilla was pleased for her, even a little envious.

When she went out to give Ben his dog biscuits he was nowhere to be seen. Clearly he had taken the invitation to sleep on the porch as an excuse to play hookey. She called a couple of times, but he didn't come.

Even without his help the cows had to be checked, and the electric fence moved; no doubt he would catch up with her somewhere around the farm, as he had once before when he had managed to slip his collar.

However, he didn't, and she began to worry.

As she filled the electric kettle for morning tea the sound of a car coming up the drive drew her attention. Her mouth trembled as she recognised Quinn's Jaguar. For a moment she allowed herself to play with the hope that he had come to explain, to give her another chance.

But the hope died, for when he got out his face was grimmer than she had ever seen it. She waited at the door, her features composed in an impassive mask. Quinn's eyes met hers, his expression so controlled that she knew it was bad news. Her heart plummeted and she went white.

'It's all right,' he said quickly, grabbing her as she sagged. 'At least—your dog has been run over.'

She was shaking her head, as if by refusing to accept it she could prevent it from being true. 'No,' she whispered. 'He wouldn't go out on the road.'

He held her gently; she could see a pulse beating in the strong brown column of his neck. 'I'm afraid he did. I found him in the ditch just below your gate. I've got him in the boot. If you tell me where you want him to go, I'll bury him.'

'But nobody came up the road last night,' she whispered. 'He couldn't have been killed then.'

He said calmly, as if she were a child, 'He's dead, Camilla. Now, tell me where you want me to bury him.'

She knew now what was meant by the last straw. After yesterday's shattering quarrel, and the long dark night of the soul she had endured since then, she had no control left. Her eyes filled with painful tears. Instantly his arms tightened, and she was hugged close to the warmth and strength of his big body. He said nothing, allowing her to weep her sorrow and shock away until she was hiccupping into his shoulder, humiliated and embarrassed.

'I'll make you some tea,' he said, his voice wonderfully gentle. 'Come into the kitchen and show me where everything is.'

Numbly she obeyed, because it was easier to do that than refuse; he was surprisingly deft, his movements swift and graceful as he moved around the tiny kitchen. After she had sipped the tea, she said, 'I'm sorry. I don't know why I cried. It's silly to get so attached to a dog . . .'

'But we all do it,' he said. 'I have a couple of spare cattle dogs. Come and see if one of them suits you.'

'I can't borrow——'

'Just until you buy one.'

'I don't really need one now, the cows are still dry.'

'You'll be able to get used to each other. When you no longer need him you can send him back. Or buy him, if you want to.' He was inexorable and, because she was tired and worried and desolated, she gave in.

'Thank you. You're very kind.'

He gave her a wry smile. 'That must have hurt. I usually am kind, it's only with you that my patience wears thin. Now, drink that up, then I'll bury Ben, and after that you can choose the dog you'd like.'

'Not today.' She looked pleadingly up at him. 'I want to—to get used to Ben not being here.'

He sent her a long, considering glance, then nodded. 'Very well. Where do you want him buried?'

She chose a spot where he used to lie and look over his domain, and sat by while Quinn dug the hole, trying not to watch the ripple of muscle beneath the thin material of his shirt as the spade rose and fell in a smooth, powerful rhythm. But when she managed to drag her eyes away from the width of his shoulders they fell helplessly on the lean, heavily muscled thighs and the play of movement in buttocks and hips as he worked.

He was all male, powerful yet gentle, dominating and protective, demanding but so confident in his own masculinity that he could celebrate the femininity of women. He didn't treat her with the essentially patronising kindness of so many men; she remembered some political discussions they'd shared, and smiled slightly as she recalled that he had given no quarter. No, a woman who was lucky enough to be loved by Quinn Fraser would be expected to be as tough-minded as he was himself.

For the first time ever Camilla acknowledged that she wanted desperately to be that woman. Which meant that not only did she want him with a devouring primitive desire that gave her no rest, but that she was in love with him.

And that, she thought drearily, was hopeless. He said he wanted her. The admission was like a breach in her barricades, but she conceded that however much he wanted the farm there was no way he could simulate his desire for her. But that was the common coinage of passion, the hunger to reproduce. She wanted more. She wanted a love as vast as hers, as impossible to contain.

And what, she asked herself, makes you think that you will succeed where others have failed, women who are much more beautiful than you, women who are sophisticated and good hostesses, as competent as his mother?

'I'll get him from the car,' he said, looking up to catch her staring at him as though she wanted to imprint his image on her mind for evermore.

Hastily she dragged her eyes away and got to her feet. At least Ben was not badly marked. She had brought the sheepskin he slept on and now she put it in the grave. Quinn lowered the dog in and she wept a little as she helped shovel the dirt back.

When it was over they went back to the house to wash their hands, and once inside Quinn said, 'Why don't you come on home?'

She essayed a sad little smile. Like this, he was very sweet, and her hungry heart was famished for crumbs. 'Thank you, but I've got work to do.'

'I can't leave you here grieving,' he said quietly. His mouth tightened. 'I had to do it once before. The time wasn't right. But I'm damned if I'm going to do it again.'

Determination was written large in his face, and meekly she went with him. He kept her with him while he worked in the office, and she spent most of the time ostensibly reading in the window-seat, but really gazing dreamily at him, her heart in her eyes. However, she insisted on going home when Karen was due back.

Karen was almost as distressed as she was over Ben's death, and even offered to stay home that evening in case she was too lonely.

'No, you go, don't be silly.' Camilla smiled at her. 'You'd upset John if you stayed home.'

Karen smiled. 'He wouldn't mind, he knows——' She hesitated, then gave a funny little shrug. 'He knows how I feel about him,' she finished.

Camilla knew, of course she did, that Karen was no longer interested in Quinn, but she found she wanted to hear it. 'And how is that?'

Karen grimaced. 'I think I'm in love with him.'

'Think?'

'Yes.' She walked across to the window, clearly searching for words. 'I've thought I was in love before, but this—this is different. This is frightening. There have been men I've wanted *as* much, but none—none I've wanted so much, if you see what I mean.'

'Yes. Yes, I think I do. This is not just physical.'

'It's much, much more than that.' Her pretty mouth firmed. 'He hasn't said anything about his first wife, only that the marriage was a mistake for both of them, but I've heard enough—well, you know how small towns are, and she must have been the world's prize bitch.'

'I don't think she was entirely normal. No, I mean that. I think she had such a massive chip on her shoulder that she needed specialist help with it.'

'Kind as ever.' Karen gave her an affectionate look. 'Was she so beautiful?'

'A dream, but no more beautiful than you are.'

'You *are* good for my morale. Well, I'm not so kind. Apparently she still tries to make his life hell, but when she has me to deal with she won't find it so easy.'

'Is she going to have you to deal with?'

Karen looked afraid for a moment. 'I hope so. He's asked me to marry him.'

'And?'

The words came out in a rush. 'Oh, Cam, I want to, more than anything I want to, but I—well, you know that I haven't lead an exactly spotless life. I wonder if perhaps he'll—he'll be repelled.'

'Don't tell him.'

Karen bit her lip. 'I'll have to.'

'Nonsense. What happened in your life before he met you is no business of his. Just as what happened to him is no business of yours. You're not going to pretend to be a virgin, are you? Well, then, all that matters is that you love him and want to make him happy.'

'Oh, Cam, sometimes I think that—I do want to make him so happy that it will make up to him for all the pain of his past, but—he deserves someone who is not——'

Camilla said fiercely. 'He deserves someone who loves him, without reservations. And who likes and respects him. That's what you deserve, too. That's all anyone can expect or deserve. Surely it's enough?'

'And you don't think I should tell him that I've been to bed with other men?'

'No. Provided you don't intend to go to bed with anyone else but him from now on.'

Karen looked horrified. 'Oh, no. Oh, I couldn't.'

'Then,' Camilla told her deliberately, 'I don't think you've got anything to worry about.'

Elation lit the golden eyes. Glowing, she said in her sweetest, most seductive voice, 'I'm going to say yes tonight, so don't worry if I don't come home. I wanted to take it slowly—it was so important, but it's been hell. I'm not made for restraint. I'm not going to bother with it from now on.' Her expression altered. 'You won't be afraid by yourself?'

'No. If anyone comes around I'll just ring Quinn and shoot the intruder at the same time!'

So Karen left looking radiant, with a charmed and charming John, who wore the bemused expression of a man who wasn't quite able to grasp his luck, and Camilla read until nine, when, suddenly exhausted, she went to bed. She lay for a little while thinking that she was happy for Karen, of course she was, but she was going to miss her.

From there her mind drifted to Ben, and tears stung her eyes. That led, inevitably, to thoughts of Quinn. She was, she admitted, envious of that incandescent happiness of Karen's, because she wanted it for herself. She wanted to revel in her love; she wanted to know that he loved her with all his heart and soul, unconditionally, wildly, as passionately as she loved him. She wanted Quinn to fall head over heels in love with her and not care about the farm at all. She wanted to live with him for the rest of their lives together. She wanted all sorts of impossible, wonderful, dangerous things...

Dreaming wistfully, she drifted off to sleep.

She never knew what it was that woke her, but she knew better than to make any noise. Motionless in the bed, she lay with eyes clamped shut while her ears strained and every instinct screamed a warning.

She could hear nothing beyond the soft wind in the trees outside. For long moments she lay there until she almost convinced herself that she was still suffering from the effects of the incident with the prowler.

Then it came again, a slight grating sound. Fear leapt into her stomach, nauseating her. This was no night noise, this was alien. And it came from within the house. She formed an image of someone moving slowly, silently through the unknown rooms, listening in case she stirred.

For long seconds she lay paralysed, but a recurrence of the soft, sinister little sound made her realise that if she was going to defend herself she couldn't afford the luxury of panic. She measured the distance to the shotgun in the wardrobe, but before she got to it he'd be in the bedroom and the element of surprise would be lost.

Now was the time to tap into the confidence that that class on self-defence had given her. Slow, deep breathing helped, as did a cool rundown on her options. It was a pity that the night was so quiet, because it meant she was going to have to stay in bed. Still, if there had been a hard wind blowing or rain falling on the corrugated-iron roof she might not have woken.

The balance of power lay very slightly with her. She was strong, and she was not afraid to hurt whoever it was that crept so slowly through her house. The initiative had been taken from his hands.

Her fear was still there, part of the adrenalin rush, but now it was controlled by her will. Forcing herself to roll over naturally, she took up a position on her back. The tiny noise stopped. She lay tensely beneath the covers, breathing carefully, her decisions made.

After what seemed to her hours, the little shuffle began again. It seemed closer this time, just outside her door. She forced herself to relax.

She heard him as soon as he came into the room. Unlike her, he was unable to control his breathing, and this small thing gave her a great surge of confidence. He paused just inside the door for long moments. Her skin prickled; she felt his eyes rove her form in the big bed, and wondered feverishly if she seemed relaxed enough. Her body was stiff, a dead giveaway. Surely he could sense her alertness, the panic she held so tightly clamped?

She almost screamed when he resumed his approach. Her eyes were by now fully adjusted to the darkness, so that beneath her lashes she could discern his outline, a darker mass against the darkness, the pale blob of his face above his dark clothes. The sound of his breathing was harsh in her ears. She thought she could smell him, and realised that he was excited and sweating.

Every nerve stretched almost to pain, she watched from beneath lowered lashes as he came to a halt and bent over her. Just a little closer, she encouraged him silently, keeping her eyes still in case he noticed the movement. Her hands lay curled, one on the pillow beside her head, the other outside the sheets.

CHAPTER NINE

EXCRUCIATINGLY slowly, the intruder's hands inched down towards Camilla's throat. Just before they reached it her right arm slashed up to jab him under the nose with the heel of her palm. There was a satisfying thunk as he gasped and swore, but before he had time to jerk his head out of reach she followed up with a fierce blow from the side of her stiffened hand to the carotid artery in his neck. He crumpled, and fell across her. Almost gagging with repulsion, she dragged in a deep, laboured breath, scrabbling frantically to free herself of her loathsome burden.

Sheer disgust gave her the strength to throw him off. He thumped on to the floor, lying in an inert heap. For a moment she wondered if she had killed him, but above the sound of her thudding heart she heard him moan.

Still high on adrenalin, she raced out of bed and flipped the light switch. Nothing happened. Half sobbing, she grabbed the torch and ran into the kitchen. Of course she couldn't find the string in the usual place, and she was almost in tears before she ran the ball to earth in the next drawer down. Terrified that he would wake and come after her, she juggled it and the scissors as she snatched them up and ran back to the bedroom.

Half-way there it occurred to her that she could leave him and run for Falls and safety; for a moment she faltered. The temptation to hand over to Quinn was well nigh irresistible, but if she left him there the intruder might wake and get away. Filled with a righteous rage that insisted he pay for his persecution, she firmed her mouth and crept noiselessly down the dark passage.

She stopped in the doorway, flicking the torch on for a second, enough for her to pick out the heap on the floor. Nevertheless, remembering her own ambush, she approached him carefully until stertorous breathing convinced her that he was still unconscious. She was not surprised to see that it was the sacked driver, all his flashy good looks gone as he lay slack-jawed and unconscious.

The idea of touching him made her shudder with disgust, but she forced herself to roll him over so that she could tie his thumbs together behind his back. And because his heavy breathing worried her, she heaved him around until she had him in as close an approximation of the recovery position as she could manage. As she did so she heard an engine coming up the road and whispered a fervent thanks. By now she was trembling with reaction, her nightgown sticking clammily to her body.

But it wasn't Karen and John. Waiting tensely in the kitchen, she heard the engine switch off and the thud of rapid booted feet on the path to the house. Quinn called, 'Camilla! Open up, Camilla.'

Shaking, her skin cold with reaction, she opened the door and fell into his arms, clutching him wildly.

'What's the matter?' he demanded, his voice almost desperate as he dragged her against him.

'Thank God, you're here,' she babbled, burrowing into the hard, warm safety of his body. 'I was going to ring— there's a man in the bedroom. I knocked him out.'

He spat a curse and held her painfully tight, his eyes stabbing through the darkness. 'Are you all right? Did he hurt you?'

'No. I heard him in the passage and I was ready for him.' But she couldn't stop trembling. 'And the power's off.'

'It's not at home. Where's you're fuse-box?'

'On the wall outside the back door.'

He went out, but was back immediately. 'The fuse is gone, removed. Darling, go and sit in the car, I'll deal with him.'

'It's the driver.'

He swore again, then said in a voice so cold that she was seared by it, 'I'll see to it that he doesn't ever look at you again. Ring—no, your phone's off.'

'No, it isn't. They fixed it. I was talking to Joe on it just before I went to bed.'

'It's off,' he said, terrifyingly expressionless. 'I suppose that bastard in there cut it again.'

She gaped. 'Again?'

'Yes. That's why I came over. The Telecom linesman noticed that the break in the line didn't seem to be in a place where it could have been done naturally. It didn't occur to them that anyone would have done it deliberately, but one of them got to thinking about it, and rang you. When he couldn't get through, he was worried enough to contact me, thank God. I—well, I'd been a little uneasy all evening so I decided to come straight down.'

'I see,' she said slowly, and shivered. 'What time is it?'

'Barely eleven o'clock.' He dropped a kiss on to her mouth, swift and starved, and ordered, 'Wait in the car.'

'No. I want to stay with you.'

She felt his resistance, but after a second he said, 'Very well. Bring the torch.'

In the bedroom the man was stirring and moaning. Quinn dropped to his knees beside him and checked the makeshift bonds. Silhouetted by the torch beam, his profile was ominously forbidding, hinting at the rage just below the surface and the immense control he was exerting to keep it there. His fingers moved, and the man gave a high-pitched moan and his head jerked back.

'You did a good job,' Quinn said, his steady tone completely at odds with that implacable expression. 'I'll keep you in mind if I ever need a bodyguard.'

He stood up and bent over to haul the intruder to his feet. Almost entirely supporting him, he dragged him out of the room and through the house, flinging commands over his shoulder as he went. 'Get some clothes on, then write a note to Karen telling her that you'll be spending the rest of the night at Falls,' he ordered.

Hastily she huddled into jeans and a polo-necked jersey, and pulled on her shoes. When she was ready Quinn was waiting beside the bench in the kitchen, his face austerely carved in bronze. 'Are you all right?'

She nodded and walked straight into his arms, hugging him in a desperate need for reassurance and comfort. 'Yes. Quinn, do you think he killed Ben?'

He held her in a bruising embrace. Into her hair he said, 'Yes, it seems too much of a coincidence, although we'll probably never be able to prove it.'

'I wish I'd hurt him even more,' she said fiercely.

He laughed softly. 'You did a damned good job. What woke you?'

'I don't know.' She shivered, recalling the fear and the panic. His arms tightened again, and he kissed her hair. 'I could hear a funny little noise. He must have been out in the hall when I woke. I knew I didn't have a hope of getting to the gun, so I had to come up with some other scheme. A few years ago I went to a self-defence class, and fortunately I wasn't too scared to remember some of the things I learnt then.'

'Not many women would have the guts to lie there and wait for him to come right up to the bed.'

'I was terrified, but there was nothing else I could do. And I somehow knew you'd come.'

'You didn't need me, you dealt more than satisfactorily with him yourself.'

Cleansed by terror, the fears and worries, the prejudices and guilt meant nothing now. She looked up into his face, her expression totally open, and said, simply, 'I'll always need you.'

Something feral and exciting leapt in his eyes. 'Good,' he said crisply. 'I was just about running out of patience. And you wait until now to tell me, when we have to deal with this——' He called the man a name Camilla could never remember actually having heard before, his voice savage with the ferocity which Karen had had so much fun fantasising over. Only this was real, this was a primitive lust for blood and he was having great difficulty controlling it.

But he kissed her, deep and slow, and when she lifted her head and gazed at him with soft, dazzled eyes, he said quietly, urgently, 'Remember, you belong to me. I've waited all my life for you, and I don't want to have to breach any more barricades later, after we've got this out of the way. Have you written a note to Karen?'

She looked a little self-conscious. 'I have, but I don't think—she didn't plan to come home tonight.'

'John McLean?' At her nod he said curtly, 'I hope she knows what she's doing. He's already been through more than any man should suffer.'

She loved him for his compassion, and hoped Karen wasn't going to be angry as she told him, 'I think they're getting engaged tonight.'

His frown lightened. 'Excellent! They're ideally suited. Now, come on. You need something to stop that shivering.'

He had put the intruder in the boot, saying grimly when, aghast, Camilla remonstrated, 'He'll be all right. It's only a short distance.'

She was still shaking violently, more, she thought, at his implacable tone than from shock, when they arrived at Falls to a reception committee of Dean and the station manager. Quinn flung his car keys at the manager and said curtly, 'Get him out and bring him in. I'll keep an eye on him until Dave Reynolds gets here.'

In the office Camilla collapsed into a chair while Quinn poured her a large glass of brandy. She sipped at it, then put it to one side, asking the first question that came to mind. 'Is your mother not here?'

'Drink it,' he said. 'You're still shivering. No, she's in Auckland. Are you sure you want to stay in this room? Perhaps it would be better if you waited upstairs.'

'No.' She took another sip, and said with painful honesty, 'I want to be here, otherwise I'll feel that he— that he's damaged me somehow. I know it sounds silly...'

He said calmly, 'I understand perfectly, though the protective instincts I'm not supposed to feel are outraged. I think you should stay if you feel up to it.'

But she had to brace herself when the men brought the driver in. He was fully conscious by now, looking about him with angry bewilderment. When he saw her that expression was replaced by frustration and malice, then the hunted fury of a cornered animal.

The men sat him down on a chair. Quinn said in a perfectly pleasant voice, 'Thank you. Wait outside, will you? And let me know when Dave arrives.'

He moved across to the telephone and rang through to the police station. In a few crisp sentences he told Dave what had happened, and hung up. 'He's on his way,' he said.

The man in the chair protested hoarsely, 'You've got no right to do this to me.'

'Really?' Quinn's voice was even, his face impassive, but the muscles in the man's throat moved as he swallowed.

'I haven't done anything. I didn't hurt her.'

'Breaking and entering will be the least charge, I imagine. What did you plan to do once you'd throttled her into submission?'

'Nothing that you haven't already done,' he retorted insolently.

Quinn's face hardened into granite. 'And how,' he asked in the silky voice of extreme rage, 'do you know that?'

'I watched you. You were with her for over an hour the other night. Plenty of time.'

Camilla gasped and the man's dogged, snarling eyes swung to her face. 'Everybody knows,' he said hoarsely. 'Everybody knows what widows are. I didn't see any reason why I shouldn't have her too. She wanted me. Didn't you, you bitch? Did she tell you that she begged me for it when I brought the metal? I'll bet she didn't. Tonight she kissed me and spread her legs for me; it was only when she heard your car coming that she got frightened, and before I knew where I was she attacked me.'

Outrage and anger almost took the top of Camilla's head off. She gasped, saying in a shaken voice, 'You're lying!'

'Prove it,' he said coarsely, showing his teeth.

'If she asked you in, why did you find it necessary to take out the fuse and cut the telephone line? And kill the dog.' Quinn's voice was coolly objective.

Camilla felt the blood ice in her veins. A shattered glance at Quinn's face revealed nothing; his face was carved in copper and she was terrified that some of the poison the man was spewing forth would reach its target.

'I didn't.' The man grinned cockily. 'Your word against mine, mate, and a hell of a court case. Both your names spread across the gutter press. The glorious name of Fraser tarnished by association with a slut.'

Very softly Quinn said, 'If that happens, if you so much as mention Camilla's name or try to pour your foul slime over her, I'll hunt you down across the world, if I have to, and hell will not be big enough to hold us both. Remember that.'

It was the last thing he said before the local policeman came in the door, and, by the expression on the other man's face, he was thinking seriously about the implications of Quinn's statement. The bravado and bluster were replaced by uneasiness; he sat with his eyes darting from Quinn to the floor, ignoring Camilla.

Camilla's blood had run cold at the calmly delivered threat. As unnerved as the intruder by the icy menace in the words, she, too, kept stealing little furtive glances at him.

Fortunately Dave arrived almost immediately, and after listening to Camilla's halting story asked her to come down to the station the next morning. Soon after she found herself sitting in the big kitchen at Falls, slowly sipping hot milk liberally laced with the rest of the brandy.

In a tone that she strove to make objective, she said, 'He can't make that—that farrago of lies stick, can he?'

'Not a hope.' Quinn's voice was infinitely reassuring. 'He won't even try. Don't worry about it.'

She whispered, 'It was so ugly.' Her gaze lifted, clung to his. 'I don't want your name brought into this.'

'It won't be.' He hesitated, then came over and sat down beside her. 'However, just in case he's stupid enough to try to convince a jury, I think you'd better marry me.'

Sheer shock rendered her numb. The milk and brandy mixture was sickly on her tongue, but she drank it to the end. Then she asked on a soft breath, 'Why?'

'Because if his spite overcomes his common sense, our marriage will refute any allegation he makes.'

Her heart broke, quite distinctly. Like someone learning to speak again, she had to pronounce every word with great care. 'It seems a rather extreme way to guard your reputation.'

He swore beneath his breath. 'I'm not worried about my reputation. If we marry, no one will believe a word he says—if he says anything.'

In a stifled voice she said, 'That's very kind of you, but I can't——'

'I might have known!' Each goaded word came out like a bullet. He came towards her, big and dominating, anger radiating from every square inch of him. 'To hell with your reputation! And mine. I don't give a damn for either. Face it, Camilla, I'm not going to let you get away. From now on your place is with me. I've given you time—three long, eternal years! I've forced myself to wait, to hold back; every day of those years I've told myself you weren't ready! God knows, I've used up all the patience I possess.'

His voice was totally without expression and his face could have been sculpted in granite. His steely will blazed forth, frightening her.

Desperately trying to infuse a thread of common sense into the exchange, she said, 'You don't have to marry me to protect me!'

'I am going to marry you because you belong to me. You belonged to me the first time I saw you,' he said deliberately. 'I fell in love with you then.'

Bewilderment froze her pale features. 'But I was married.'

'Yes.' His smile was a travesty, angry and self-derisory. 'An amusing situation for a sophisticated man to find himself in. The only woman I have ever wanted to marry, and you were already married. For the first time in my life I saw a woman I would kill for. And she was the bride of another man.'

She stood up abruptly, trying to convince herself that they were really having this conversation. 'You can't fall in love at first sight.'

'I know.' He looked down at her with hooded eyes and gave a short, humourless laugh. 'I told myself that, too. I even believed it. You looked like a fairy. Oh, not the gauzy artificial ones in bad fairy-tales, but the real sort, ones from myth and legend, wild and more than a little dangerous, perhaps even a little cruel, with your eyes set on a slant and your pale skin like silk and your red, passionate mouth. Yet you were so polite, so sweetly deferential to everyone. I wanted to know if that perilous gleam I caught in your incredible eyes was real, or if it came from my imagination. Unfortunately, closer acquaintance only convinced me that if it wasn't love at first sight, it was at second. You knew, too.'

'No! I didn't——' Her voice broke. She stared at him, and saw the mockery in his smile, and realised that he was right. In a whisper she said, 'I didn't understand.'

'I know that. You are loyal—the thought of wanting anyone other than your husband filled you with such guilty dismay that you repressed it completely. Unfortunately I wasn't able to do that. I had to go away.'

She sat down heavily again into the chair, staring blindly at her hands. The long fingers trembled then stilled. 'When you went I felt—bereft,' she admitted for the very first time. 'And guilty. I didn't know why.'

'I wanted to snatch you away from Dave. I couldn't bear—I tried not to think of him taking you, making love to you. It caught in my gut, made me burn with a fire that was going to destroy us all.' His voice was flat, unemotional, yet she could see the effort it was costing him to keep it like that.

'Especially,' he went on, 'as I wondered if perhaps it was just infatuation, an obsession. I didn't want to fall in love with you. Until then married women had been strictly out of bounds. I resented the power you wielded, even though it was patently, painfully obvious that you were completely unconscious of it. So I decided to go away, give this bloody inconvenient passion a chance to fade. And if it didn't, the interval would give you the chance to see for yourself that your marriage to Dave wasn't going to work out.'

He gave a twisted smile in which she could see some of the torment he had suffered. 'Only it didn't die. I couldn't breathe or eat or sleep properly without you beside me. The need for you was in my heart and my mind and my loins. When I came back it was to take

you away from Dave. And Dave knew it. He'd sensed
it right from the start.'

She lifted eyes that were filled with pain, bleakly accepting. 'Was *that* why he hated you? But how could he
know? When I didn't know myself what I was feeling,
how could he?'

'Intuition, I suppose. He loved you, and he was as
territorial as I am. That was how my mother described
it.'

Camilla coloured and lowered her head. 'Your
mother?'

'It was she who suggested I leave.' His voice
roughened. 'I wanted to take you with me, but she said
you weren't ready, that if I broke up your marriage you
would never be able to trust yourself again. Was she
right, Camilla? Or were these last three years just
wasted?'

She bit her lip. After a ragged pause, she said reluctantly, 'No. I was beginning to see for myself, and then
Dave died. I was confused, because you're right, I've
always been aware of you. As though there was something that linked us, and yet it seemed so—presump-
tuous of me.'

'No, oh, no, my dearest.' If she hadn't believed him
before she would have known that he loved her by the
tone of his voice, deep and unbearably moved.

Tears filled her eyes, but she said unevenly, 'I wish
we hadn't hurt Dave. I married him because I was lonely.
My mother died, and Uncle Philip left me the farm, and
Dave suggested we get married. I should never have
agreed. I short-changed him.'

'He married you as a way to achieve his ambition.'
The words were cut off, harsh. 'Dreams have to be
worked for, Camilla. He used you as a short cut.'

She bit her lip. 'I feel so guilty because I didn't love him as much as he loved me,' she said sadly.

'Yes. You have a propensity for guilt. It worked very well for him.'

Camilla gave a bleak little smile. 'You're too hard on him. It doesn't alter the fact that I married him for all the wrong reasons.'

'Perhaps, although any man who marries a very young woman still grieving for the only parent she has ever known can't really blame her if things work out poorly.'

His harshness upset her enough to make the look that came his way uncertain and a little remote.

He gave a kind of grimace. 'Yes, I know, that's not fair. Unfortunately when I think of him jealousy gets in the way of common sense. I'll probably always be angry that we had to wait. When it comes to you, my body and my heart seem to take over from my mind. I've always been rather proud of my detachment, and your effect on it gives you the sort of power that frightens me.'

'I'm afraid of it, too. I saw what that kind of love did to my mother; she faded away after my father died, and I suppose that deep down I didn't want to face that kind of pain. I've come to think that perhaps that's why I married Dave, because I sensed that he would never affect me like that.' Her mouth twisted. 'It was foolish and bad. If I'd been a little more honest about myself, Dave might be alive today.'

He leaned over and spoke forcefully. 'If Dave had spent some money fitting a frame to the tractor, he would be alive today. Don't go wallowing in even more guilt.'

Unwillingly she told him of her deepest fear. 'I wondered—if, when he knew that I wasn't—that I didn't really love him—whether perhaps he just didn't care enough to take precautions.'

'Stop that!' At last he did what she had been longing for, reached out and without ceremony pulled her into his arms. They closed around her with satisfying strength as he commanded, 'You are not to do this to yourself! He wanted to live as much as any other man. He didn't put a canopy on the tractor because he was sure he'd never have an accident. Yes, he loved you, and he hated the thought of me taking you, but he was quite confident that he had you tied to him in every way that mattered. And because you're so loyal he could well have been right. I was afraid of that. I was banking on the fact that as well as that burnished loyalty you have passion he hadn't even touched. I planned to do so.'

His mouth touched hers, gently at first, but as soon as he felt her incandescent response the kiss deepened as though he had starved for her over long years. A shudder of delight ran through her, setting her alight, forming traceways of sensation from her feet right up to her scalp. Heat seared her skin, and she shivered as tiny beads of moisture prickled across her brow. Her mouth opened, accommodated the fierce thrust of his tongue, and reciprocated with a wildness she didn't recognise in herself.

A long time later, when her whole being was afire for him, he rested his forehead on hers and said thickly, 'My dearest love, my darling girl, if you want to finish this conversation I think you had better do it quickly. I want no hangovers from the past shadowing our love.'

Touched, she kissed along the stark line of his jaw, revelling in the contrast of beard against smooth skin, then said dreamily, 'I thought you just wanted the farm.'

'But I do,' he said promptly. 'Life doesn't come finished in neat little compartments, Camilla. I still want it. No one else is going to be a thorn in my side, as Philip and Dave were.'

'I'm not,' she said, stung.

He gave her a glittering smile. 'Darling, you were a thorn in my heart. I hoped that I might be able to persuade you to love me, even if you didn't really trust me. I wanted that surrender, the trust that goes beyond reason. And in the end you gave it to me.'

She nodded. 'If only we'd been frank with each other...'

'I've never gone for the easy option. I had to know that you trust me, and I think you had to know that I wasn't like Dave, loving you, but using you as a stepping-stone to an ambition. We both wanted proof, but when the crunch came we took each other on trust. Do what you want with the farm. Give it to our children,' he said negligently.

Her heart thudding in her breast, she raised her lashes; what she saw made her heart thunder in her chest.

Narrowed eyes, brilliant beneath his heavy lids, a mouth that was thin with control. He looked like a hunter when the prey to which he had devoted his life, which he knew better than himself, was at last within his reach. He looked like a man who had walked in the shadows all his life, then was at last given the gift of sunshine. Fear, and expectation so intense that it was like a pain, warred in her breast. She wanted him, and at last it seemed to her that she was free to take, to give all that she was and take all that he was. But first she had to lower the last barriers.

She said, 'Uncle Philip said you were totally unscrupulous. That's why I was so suspicious. I thought you were flirting with me to try to persuade me to sell to you. I let you do it, because I wanted to—to be close to you, even if it was false. That's why I didn't tell you about the will; I thought if you knew it was impossible you might leave me alone, and I wanted to see you so much! But I felt so guilty, so dirty for wanting you. It was as though I betrayed both Dave and my uncle. So whenever I did see you I backed away, trying to convince myself that I hated you.'

He said something short and rude. The predatory look had faded slightly, but his arrogant features still revealed the knife-edge of need. Camilla rejoiced, knowing that the same seeking hunger was there for him to see in her face, too.

'Stop looking at me like that,' he said unevenly. 'Or be prepared to take the consequences.'

As calmly as she could, she said, 'I didn't hate you, of course.'

'I knew that,' he said, infuriating her with his high-handed confidence. He laughed at the expression on her face, but went on. 'Everything conspired against us. Even Karen, although she made it easier for me to get close to you. If she hadn't come you'd have gone on refusing invitations, and I'd have had to be even more brutal than I was. You just about drove me mad! I could see what you were thinking—or trying to persuade yourself to think.'

'Between you and Karen, I've been forced to think very seriously about what I was doing. I'd been refusing to face any issues, hiding away from reality—I'm very good at that. But tonight while I lay in bed waiting for a man who could conceivably kill me, who certainly wanted to humiliate and rape me, I thought that I wouldn't let another day go past without telling you that

I love you. I realised that we have no guarantees. I should
have understood that when Dave was killed, but I refused to face that, too.' Very shyly she looked up at him.
'Quinn, are you really sure?'

He extended his hand, all supreme masculine confidence. 'I have never been surer of anything in my life.
You're going to marry me as soon as possible. In the
meantime, however, do you want us to wait?'

Slowly, because he wasn't going to do it for her, she
reached out. His hand engulfed hers, very big, lean and
strong and warm. He exerted a little pressure, drawing
her smoothly up into the strong cage of his arms.

She looked up, apprehension darkening her eyes. She
could deny him nothing, but honesty forced an
admission.

'I'm not very good at making love,' she said softly.

Fascinated, she watched the tiny muscles along his
jawbone clench. 'I don't believe that, my heart. The few
times we've kissed, we set the world on fire.'

'I mean—I didn't—I don't know very much. I——'
She couldn't continue because her mouth had dried up
completely.

'Shall we see?'

Swallowing hard, she nodded, but before his mouth
could seal off the words she said desperately, 'And if I
don't—if I don't satisfy you, then you don't—I mean,
you don't have to marry me.'

The words finished on a rush. He kissed her pleading
eyes closed and said very softly. 'Sex is not the only thing,
my sweet enchantress. I'd marry you if you were in a
wheelchair and all that I could do to you was kiss you.
Now, see if you can relax...'

His mouth was sweet as wine, intoxicating as strong
rum. In the secret reaches of the night when she had

wondered what he would be like as a lover and fantasised a little, she had imagined that he would be fiercely ardent. The edge of violence in him was well controlled, but, like Karen, she had always recognised it.

But this time he kissed her softly, seducing the tension from her until she was pliable and melting in his arms. Still kissing her, he picked her up and took her through the door and along the dim hall to the stairs.

'Put me down,' she whispered. 'I'm too heavy!'

She could feel his laughter in his chest as he set her on her feet. With his arm around her shoulder they walked side by side up the curving staircase, and along the hall. His bedroom was the master suite, huge and shadowy, decorated in the grand style with a sumptuous four-poster bed four-square to the wall.

Camilla hid her nervousness by saying on a sudden indrawn breath. 'No wonder you have such an air of the grand seigneur!'

'If you don't like it you can banish it to the attics.'

She turned a horrified face to him, but her assurance that she would never do such a thing was lost under the warm, coaxing pressure of his mouth. On a gasping little sob she flung her arm around him, yielding with an eagerness that could not be suppressed.

When the kiss ended and she was looking at him with sultry, slumbrous eyes, he turned her around and bit the nape of her neck, not too hard, just enough for delicious little chills to run up and down her spine.

Her jersey was eased free; he pulled it over her head and she realised that he had unclipped her bra. She wanted so badly to look desirable for him; it seemed unfair that she should be wearing her oldest bra and faded jeans, but he was gazing at her as though he saw all heaven in his arms.

The sinuous little shudders caused by his strong teeth on her unprotected nape were joined by others that had their birth deep in the pit of her stomach. Swaying into his arms, she nuzzled his neck, breathing deeply so that she could take in his warm male essence, mysterious and beloved, his particular scent. His skin was hot and smooth, and she kissed his throat, delighted and stimulated when he groaned and his arms tightened about her.

Heady fumes began to join with the turmoil in her nervous system to cloud her brain; emboldened by his reaction, her fingers lingered over the hardness of the muscles in his back, and slid down to his buttocks. The long muscles there locked and, alarmed, she looked up. His face was drawn, the skin pulled sharply over the magnificent bone-structure, but she read his pleasure in his eyes, and her mouth curved in a slow, feline smile of complete understanding. Her blood began to sing in her veins. She ran her hands up his back, feeling the muscles shift and tense beneath her seeking palms, and suddenly she wanted his weight on her, to be pinned beneath him, vulnerable, open, naked in voluptuous helplessness.

'Oh, God,' he muttered, watching the shifting patterns in her face, the heat kindling in her eyes, darkening the palely luminous colour into a blaze. 'Camilla—I need you so much!'

His mouth was cruel, all gentleness gone, forcing hers open to receive the sudden thrust of his tongue. A thick sound escaped from her throat. She shuddered with the fire at the fork of her legs, and her hips moved in an involuntary, primal thrust against his hardened body.

After that there was no going back. Her clothes fell on to the floor and she helped him wrench his from his magnificently aroused body, her capable hands tugging at the confining material in an eagerness she no longer had to hide.

When they stood facing each other she reached out and caressed the smooth, heated bulge of muscle in his upper arm. 'You are beautiful,' she said on a sigh.

He looked at her, the milk-white skin, the long, slender silkiness of her, fragile yet strong enough to lean on, and he said, 'And you are magic. A witch-woman, an enchantress from faerie.'

Her face was dazzled. She touched her tongue to her lower lip and, as if the tiny movement was the thing that broke his self-control, he reached blindly for her and picked her up and carried her across the room to the bed.

The sheets were cool and soothing to her back. She went down with her arms held out, glad that the light was still on and they could see each other, glad that she lay exposed to him in the position that had always been faintly humiliating before. But when she expected him to move over her he lay beside her and stroked her with a hand that trembled. Dark skin against pale, long, strong fingers against the delicacy of her woman's curves, the power of his strength kept at bay by the weakness of her femininity; a tide swirled over her, gold and red, and she succumbed with more than a muted murmur to the caress of his hands, his mouth, the ways of love that she had never before experienced.

She was transcended from selfhood, beyond personality, yet never so vividly, fiercely Camilla, who loved and was loved, who lay moaning in an agony that was beyond pleasure.

When at last he took her she cried out, and he said harshly, 'Am I hurting?'

'No.' She tried to tell him that she was burning with pleasure, imprisoned in and dying of it, only the words wouldn't come.

But he understood because he gave her a feral grin, his expression almost as agonised as hers, and began to move, the strong body invading hers, taking it over, and yet being engulfed by her. She discovered that there were pleasures past pleasures, that choking whispers could express an excitement beyond words. She heard herself moaning as waves of ecstasy centred in on her, throwing her up through a maelstrom of sensation that built again and threw her further, and further, until at last it imploded in a rapturous ecstasy, and she lay holding him in her arms as they dragged in breath enough to keep them conscious.

Whispering his name, she burst into tears.

He rolled over and cuddled her against him, his hand stroking her hair back from her face while she wept as though her heart would break.

When she had quietened down he said raggedly, 'Too much of that will kill us both.'

Colour flooded her skin. She whispered. 'I didn't know...'

Very tenderly he lifted her face, his eyes searching out hers. 'Neither did I. I have never felt such—it was a completely new experience for me, too, Camilla, my sweet Camilla, my dearest lady, my lovely girl. I love you.'

'I love you.' She kissed his throat. 'I've cried all over you. I honestly thought I was going to die.'

'Me, too. Everything I've done, every day of my life up until now, was the prelude to that. But the wonderful thing, the marvellous thing, is that there are going to be other wonderful days and nights, other experiences...

I want to swim naked with you in the pool at the falls. I want to watch you in the shower, and on a beach, and in the moonlight, with the moon silvering that lovely body.' He laughed and kissed the point of her shoulder. 'I want to wake up at three o'clock in the morning and hear your breathing, and touch you, and feel you come alive against my hand. Think of all the things we have to discover about each other! And all the years we'll have to do it in.'

She blushed and kissed his chest, and blushed again, because his hand was roving, pushing up the soft globes of her breasts, stroking gently over her peaking nipples.

Just before she surrendered to the tide of desire that had begun to gather, as thick as honey in her veins, she asked, 'Quinn, did you ring the bank manager and guarantee the loan I had to take out to pay for the repairs to the culvert?'

His hand stilled. 'What makes you think that?' But his voice was so non-committal that he gave himself away.

'Because he shouldn't have given me a loan. Looked at from his point of view, I'm a very poor risk. And when he was talking to whoever was on the other end, he was looking at me in a funny way; vague, yet speculative. I refused to think about it—I'm good at hiding from unpleasant facts—but lately I've become almost sure. It was you, wasn't it?'

His hand moved slowly across the tight buds of her breasts, stimulating skin that was already almost unbearably sensitive from the ministrations of his mouth.

After a moment he said on a note of amusement, 'I can see I'm not going to be able to hide anything from you. Yes, I did. And I'm not in the least sorry. I also told Dean I'd pay him any extra above a certain amount when he worked on the tractor.'

She laughed, a husky little sound, and inclined her head to touch her tongue to the tiny male nipples, rejoicing as they copied the unbearably sensuous flowering of her own. His indrawn breath was heaven to her ears. 'Somehow I'm finding it very difficult to be suitably angry with you,' she said demurely.

He laughed beneath his breath and ran his hand from her breast to her waist, and down the long, lovely line of her hip to come to rest on the smooth expanse of her thigh. She thought fancifully that she could feel his touch in every cell of her body, every single nerve, rejoicing at this overwhelming possession.

Throatily, she whispered, 'I don't care any more.'

He understood what she was trying to say. It was all over. She would never feel guilty again, because no one had the right to demand a promise from beyond the grave. Dave and her uncle were at rest, and she and Quinn were alive and in love, and loving. They had their lives to live, without interference or harassment from the past.

So in laughter and in love they made their peace with the past, and looked to a future that stretched glowing with promise before them.

Harlequin Presents®

Coming Next Month

HARLEQUIN
American Romance®

November brings you ...

SENTIMENTAL JOURNEY

BARBARA BRETTON

Jitterbugging at the Stage Door Canteen, singing along with the Andrews Sisters, planting your Victory Garden—this was life on the home front during World War II.

Barbara Bretton captures all the glorious memories of America in the 1940's in SENTIMENTAL JOURNEY—a nostalgic Century of American Romance book and a Harlequin Award of Excellence title.

Available wherever Harlequin® books are sold.

ARE YOU A ROMANCE READER WITH OPINIONS?

Openings are currently available for participation in the 1990-1991 Romance Reader Panel. We are looking for new participants from all regions of the country and from all age ranges.

If selected, you will be polled once a month by mail to comment on new books you have recently purchased, and may occasionally be asked for more in-depth comments. Individual responses will remain confidential and all postage will be prepaid.

Regular purchasers of one favorite series, as well as those who sample a variety of lines each month, are needed, so fill out and return this application today for more detailed information.

1. Please indicate the romance series you purchase from regularly at retail outlets.

Harlequin	Silhouette	
1. ☐ Romance	6. ☐ Romance	10. ☐ Bantam Loveswept
2. ☐ Presents	7. ☐ Special Edition	11. ☐ Other _____
3. ☐ American Romance	8. ☐ Intimate Moments	
4. ☐ Temptation	9. ☐ Desire	
5. ☐ Superromance		

2. Number of romance paperbacks you purchase new in an average month:

   12.1 ☐ 1 to 4   .2 ☐ 5 to 10   .3 ☐ 11 to 15   .4 ☐ 16+

3. Do you currently buy romance   13.1 ☐ yes   .2 ☐ no
   series through direct mail?

   If yes, please indicate series: _____
                                                           (14,15)   (16,17)

4. Date of birth: _____ / _____ / _____
                  (Month) (Day) (Year)
                   18,19   20,21   22,23

5. Please print:
   Name: _____
   Address: _____
   City: _____ State: _____ Zip: _____
   Telephone No. (optional): (_____) _____

MAIL TO: Attention: Romance Reader Panel
         Consumer Opinion Center
         P.O. Box 1395
         Buffalo, NY 14240-9961   ☐☐☐☐☐☐☐☐☐☐☐☐☐

                                         Office Use Only   HPDK

Take 4 bestselling love stories FREE

Plus get a FREE surprise gift!

PASSPORT TO ROMANCE
SWEEPSTAKES RULES

1. **HOW TO ENTER:** To enter, you must be the age of majority and complete the official entry form, or print your name, address, telephone number and age on a plain piece of paper and mail to: Passport to Romance, P.O. Box 9056, Buffalo, NY 14269-9056. No mechanically reproduced entries accepted.

2. All entries must be received by the CONTEST CLOSING DATE, DECEMBER 31, 1990 TO BE ELIGIBLE.

3. **THE PRIZES:** There will be ten (10) Grand Prizes awarded, each consisting of a choice of a trip for two people from the following list:
   i)   London, England (approximate retail value $5,050 U.S.)
   ii)   England, Wales and Scotland (approximate retail value $6,400 U.S.)
   iii) Carribean Cruise (approximate retail value $7,300 U.S.)
   iv)   Hawaii (approximate retail value $9,550 U.S.)
   v)   Greek Island Cruise in the Mediterranean (approximate retail value $12,250 U.S.)
   vi)   France (approximate retail value $7,300 U.S.)

4. Any winner may choose to receive any trip or a cash alternative prize of $5,000.00 U.S. in lieu of the trip.

5. **GENERAL RULES:** Odds of winning depend on number of entries received.

6. A random draw will be made by Nielsen Promotion Services, an independent judging organization, on January 29, 1991, in Buffalo, NY, at 11:30 a.m. from all eligible entries received on or before the Contest Closing Date.

7. Any Canadian entrants who are selected must correctly answer a time-limited, mathematical skill-testing question in order to win.

8. Full contest rules may be obtained by sending a stamped, self-addressed envelope to: "Passport to Romance Rules Request", P.O. Box 9998, Saint John, New Brunswick, Canada E2L 4N4.

9. Quebec residents may submit any litigation respecting the conduct and awarding of a prize in this contest to the Régie des loteries et courses du Québec.

10. Payment of taxes other than air and hotel taxes is the sole responsibility of the winner.

11. Void where prohibited by law.

COUPON BOOKLET OFFER TERMS

To receive your Free travel-savings coupon booklets, complete the mail-in Offer Certificate on the preceeding page, including the necessary number of proofs-of-purchase, and mail to: Passport to Romance, P.O. Box 9057, Buffalo, NY 14269-9057. The coupon booklets include savings on travel-related products such as car rentals, hotels, cruises, flowers and restaurants. Some restrictions apply. The offer is available in the United States and Canada. Requests must be postmarked by January 25, 1991. Only proofs-of-purchase from specially marked "Passport to Romance" Harlequin® or Silhouette® books will be accepted. The offer certificate must accompany your request and may not be reproduced in any manner. Offer void where prohibited or restricted by law. LIMIT FOUR COUPON BOOKLETS PER NAME, FAMILY, GROUP, ORGANIZATION OR ADDRESS. Please allow up to 8 weeks after receipt of order for shipment. Enter quickly as quantities are limited. Unfulfilled mail-in offer requests will receive free Harlequin® or Silhouette® books (not previously available in retail stores), in quantities equal to the number of proofs-of-purchase required for Levels One to Four, as applicable.

PR-SWPS

OFFICIAL SWEEPSTAKES
ENTRY FORM

Complete and return this Entry Form immediately—the more Entry Forms you submit, the better your chances of winning!
- Entry Forms must be received by **December 31, 1990**   3-HP-2-SW
- A random draw will take place on **January 29, 1991**
- Trip must be taken by **December 31, 1991**

YES, I want to win a PASSPORT TO ROMANCE vacation for two! I understand the prize includes round-trip air fare, accommodation and a daily spending allowance.

Name_____

Address_____

City_____ State_____ Zip_____

Telephone Number_____ Age_____

Return entries to: **PASSPORT TO ROMANCE**, P.O. Box 9056, Buffalo, NY 14269-9056

© 1990 Harlequin Enterprises Limited

COUPON BOOKLET/OFFER CERTIFICATE

Item	LEVEL ONE Booklet 1	LEVEL TWO Booklet 1 & 2	LEVEL THREE Booklet 1, 2 & 3	LEVEL FOUR Booklet 1, 2, 3 & 4
Booklet 1 = $100+	$100+	$100+	$100+	$100+
Booklet 2 = $200+		$200+	$200+	$200+
Booklet 3 = $300+			$300+	$300+
Booklet 4 = $400+				$400+
Approximate Total Value of Savings	$100+	$300+	$600+	$1,000+
# of Proofs of Purchase Required	4	6	12	18
Check One				

Name_____

Address_____

City_____ State_____ Zip_____

Return Offer Certificates to: **PASSPORT TO ROMANCE**, P.O. Box 9057, Buffalo, NY 14269-9057

Requests must be postmarked by **January 25, 1991**

ONE PROOF OF PURCHASE   3-HP-2

To collect your free coupon booklet you must include the necessary number of proofs-of-purchase with a properly completed Offer Certificate   © 1990 Harlequin Enterprises Limited

See previous page for details